THE NANNY PROPOSAL

LUCY LENNOX

Cover Design: Beetiful Book Covers
Editing: One Love Editing
Beta Reading: May Archer

THE NANNY PROPOSAL

I've been in love with Dr. Grant Brighton for four long years.

He's tall. Gorgeous. Brilliant. An amazing single dad.

He's also straight, uninterested in dating someone ten years younger than him, and, tragically, *my boss*.

If I'd known taking the nanny position would mean mangling my heart, I might never have accepted his offer, but I love the Brighton family so I've resigned myself to never living the fairytale…

At least until the Dean of Admissions at the girls' dream school says only families with two parents need apply, and in desperation, Grant makes me a different offer: to be his on-paper *husband*.

With things heating up between us and my heart hanging in the balance, how can I convince Grant to make me the proposal I really want: to turn this marriage of convenience into a real-life happily-ever-after?

1

GRANT

I was pretty sure I hadn't sat still this long since med school.

The *tick tick tick* of the grandfather clock in the corner seemed incredibly slow, dust motes whirled in the shaft of sunlight that spilled through the leaded glass window into the wood-paneled room, and despite the way the hard-backed chair had made my ass go numb, I was so sleep-deprived that I was sorely tempted to fall asleep right there in the dean of admissions' office.

"Dr. Brighton?" Dean Larson, a kindly older woman who reminded me of a Hollywood actress—I'd need to check with Brody to figure out which one—had glanced up from perusing the endless stack of paperwork we'd submitted weeks ago and was peering over her reading glasses at me from the other side of her mahogany desk as though waiting for the answer to a question.

"Hmm? Oh! Sorry. What were you saying?" I tried to look alert and engaged while also surreptitiously sneaking a peek at my phone to verify that I had no new updates from the hospital. One of my emergency surgical patients had been hypoxic when I'd left for this appointment, and I'd been tempted to cancel. But, Brody had reminded me, it had taken months to even get an interview with the Mountbatten Preparatory Academy, and it was important to make a good impression. My three girls already had friends at the elite private school, and Jacey, in particular, was desperate to join their theater program, which was "next-level, Dad."

So here I was, exhausted but earning some much-needed father points...

Though I really wished I could simply write the school a check and be done with it.

Focus, Grant.

"I was saying that your application is extremely impressive. The girls have outstanding records from their previous school, and the recommendation from Jacey's drama coach is remarkable."

I nodded. Brody had prepared everything for me, and I'd only had to sign it, therefore I was confident everything was in order.

"But I did have a question..." she continued.

I licked my lips. I could do this. I answered questions from patients and concerned loved ones every day. I could absolutely answer questions about my own children. "Right. Sure. Fire away."

"It's about Mr., ah... Brody Kelly." She nodded toward the paperwork. "He's the other person listed as the girls' emergency contact?"

"Oh. Yes. Yes, he is," I said firmly, relieved to be asked a question I knew the answer to. If she'd been asking for the girls' clothing or shoe sizes, I might have panicked like an intern presenting a patient to his attending for the first time.

Brody continually told me that it didn't matter that I didn't know Cleo's favorite lunchbox treats or whose turn it was to drive Mia's gymnastics car pool. "That's why you hired me, Dr. Brighton. Remember?" he'd say gently, his green eyes going soft. "It's way more important that you're trying to make it to Friday movie nights and Jacey's lacrosse games and that you spend time talking with each of the girls every day. Focus on *that* stuff."

I wasn't sure he was right, but I really appreciated him saying so.

The dean lifted her eyebrows at me expectantly, but I wasn't sure what else I was supposed to say. "Did you... need Brody's phone number?" I guessed. "I'm pretty sure it's on the form."

"No. I wanted to know about Mr. Kelly's *relationship* to you," she prompted a bit impatiently. "Is he a family member?"

Oh.

I felt a smile tug at the corners of my lips without conscious thought.

Technically, Brody Kelly wasn't family. I'd hired him to be our live-in nanny—or, as Brody teasingly corrected me, our "full-time childcare specialist"—four years ago now at my sister's bidding, because she'd insisted I needed more support than the part-time babysitters I'd employed up to that point. But since then, he'd proven himself absolutely invaluable. The girls utterly adored him, and I...

Well. I liked him very much.

Professionally.

Because he was my employee.

And if I also had other sorts of thoughts about him—about how his eyes sparkled with happiness in a way that shouldn't have been scientifically possible, or the way a fascinating little dimple popped on his left cheek when he was truly amused, or how the sight of him coming home from the gym in sweat-soaked, ass-hugging short-shorts made my heart rate increase as though *I'd* been the one getting a workout—well, I forcibly ignored those, by mentally reciting a list of every bone in the human body, if necessary, because to do other-wise would be... *un*professional. Professionally speaking.

My cheeks went hot, and I squirmed slightly in the chair.

Occipital bone, parietal bone...

"Brody's not exactly *family*," I admitted, flustered.

But I didn't want her to think that he was just a random name I'd put down as an emergency contact, either. I wanted her to under-stand that I trusted the man implicitly to make whatever decisions were needed for the girls... So I kept talking when ordinarily I would have kept my mouth shut.

"Brody is... he's wonderful. He loves my girls so well—and I don't mean that he makes sure they get their biannual dental cleaning and brings them lemon honey tea when they have a cold." Though he did those things, too. "Brody's genuinely interested in what they have to say, and he gets enthusiastic about what they're enthusiastic about. Do you know, when Mia wanted to take up archery because she saw it in a Disney movie, Brody started taking lessons with her?" I chuckled to myself. Mia had been a quick study, but Brody's aim was objectively terrible to this day. "When Cleo became passionate about ichthyology, Brody helped her research fish tanks and got us one on Facebook Marketplace. And when Jacey's musical theater group did *Hairspray* last spring, he learned all the choreography so he could help her practice. All while managing a full college course load of his own for a software engineering degree. Brody's the best thing that ever happened to the girls and me. He's an incredible role model, and he helps me to be a better dad. So, I—" I broke off, a little horrified by my own rambling. *Shit.* I was way too tired for this meeting. "I'm so sorry. What was the question?"

Dean Larson's face had morphed from its earlier businesslike mien into something liquid-soft and approachable. It was the sort of face my girls made when Brody showed them cute kitten GIFs. The sort of face Brody himself made when we'd encountered a golden retriever puppy gamboling around the playground last Saturday. I wasn't sure what I'd said to put that *OMG-look-at-the-cuteness expression* on the dean's face.

"I think you've answered my question perfectly, Dr. Brighton." She beamed. "And, might I add, Mr. Kelly is a very lucky man to be spoken of so highly."

"Oh." I returned her smile uncertainly. "Not at all. We're the lucky ones to have him."

"That's lovely. Just lovely." She gave me a quick wink. "You know, we're supportive of all kinds of families here at Mountbatten. We embrace diversity."

I nodded. That was one of the things I'd considered carefully before agreeing to Jacey's request that we apply. I'd read several peer-reviewed journal studies about the importance of diversity to improve outcomes for children across the board, particularly with their mental health. More than that, it was something I felt strongly about on a personal level.

I hadn't figured out I was gay until surprisingly late—as in, not until five years ago, when my ex-wife had already decided she was unfulfilled by our quiet suburban life and suggested exploring what would make each of us truly happy... separately. I wasn't sure that having access to an LGBTQ+ alliance like the one Mountbatten offered back when I was in high school would have changed *that* outcome in the slightest, but it couldn't have hurt.

"We simply like to make sure that all applicants come from a family environment that will enable their families to be active in our little community," she went on. "Fundraising, intramural sports and extracurricular activities, social events... they don't just happen. To best support our children, it takes a village, Dr. Brighton."

I nodded again. "That sounds... great." In theory. "But, ah." I tugged at the collar of my button-down and considered my current patient load, which already made it tricky to get home for family dinner many nights. "What level of involvement would I be required to take on as a parent?"

"Well, obviously, we understand that many of our parents have demanding careers. As a doctor, I'm sure there'll be times when you won't be available for the girls' school events..."

"Yes." I let out a relieved breath. The last thing I wanted was for my career to hold the girls back from anything.

"...but on those occasions, they'll have their other dad here," she said brightly. "Which will be perfect."

I blinked at the dean uncomprehendingly. "Their... other dad," I repeated.

"Stepfather, bonus parent." She waved a dismissive hand. "Whatever Mr. Kelly chooses to call himself within your own family will be respected, of course."

"Mr. Kelly. Of course," I echoed faintly.

I had the sinking feeling that "full-time childcare specialist" was not going to cut it here.

I conjured an image of Brody in my mind. At twenty-four years old, he was still young—ten years younger than me—but the way he'd taken on responsibility in our household right away made it clear that he was incredibly mature for his age. More mature than I was sometimes, at least when it came to understanding the girls' needs. My sister, Gwen, often said I had a "brilliant brain for medicine that doesn't allow room for much else," which was a nicer way of saying that I was a workaholic who sucked at emotions.

When he'd moved in, Brody had been attending college nearby and had needed a position that offered room and board close to campus. But what had started out as a convenient arrangement for both of us had become so much more. He was the one the girls went to when they woke up in the middle of the night with bad dreams. He was the one who raced to school with forgotten homework and left-behind lunch boxes. He was even the one my mother called first when making plans that included us.

In many ways, I could see why he'd be mistaken for the girls' "other dad," except in the singularly most important one: Brody wasn't my husband. Not even close.

And thank god he wasn't, or, given my track record with relationships, I'd have run him off by now.

I opened my mouth to correct her assumption when Dean Larson leaned forward.

"You know," she said confidingly, "I have to admit that I was initially hesitant to admit the girls to Mountbatten. We only accept a small number of new students each year as it is, and it's so difficult to find families who don't simply want to write a check and be done with it."

"Wow." I forced a chuckle and tugged at my collar again. "That's wild. I can't imagine."

"Indeed. While we do our best to ensure that we accept a number of students from a variety of races, ethnicities, religions, socioeconomic backgrounds, academic abilities, family structures, and so on, in order to uphold our school's values, we simply must have a high level of family involvement across the board. So when I saw on your application that your stated profession is 'one of the state's most highly respected trauma surgeons'—"

Dammit, Brody.

"—and that the girls' mother is an 'award-winning photojournalist' who's currently living abroad 'capturing humanity's stories'... by the way, thank you so much for linking me to her website. It was extremely informative—"

I nodded woodenly. *Brody again.*

"—well, I was extremely impressed, but you can understand why I was concerned that your family wouldn't be capable of really taking an active role within our community. I know it might seem old-fashioned," she said earnestly, "but there are many schools in the area where parents can send their children if they're looking for rigorous, college-preparatory academics, and others where athletically gifted children can gain access to world-renowned coaches. What sets Mountbatten apart is our spirit. We *care* for one another here, Dr. Brighton. Our parents get to know their children's classmates and their classmates' parents. We function as a team. And it's really impossible to achieve that if our soccer stadium is filled with paid babysitters scrolling their phones."

"I see." I wanted to argue that not all paid caregivers were like that. That many, like Brody, were incredibly invested in their children's lives, while many of the children's parents—namely, *me*—were the ones with a phone habit to break.

But then I imagined Jacey's face when I told her I'd blown her shot at Mountbatten, and I held my tongue.

Dean Larson sat back in her seat and regarded me for a moment. "If you'd like, I can forward you some studies showing the effects that high levels of in-personal parental involvement can achieve—"

"No need," I said flatly. I'd no doubt read them all... and had been triply glad that I had someone like Brody in my corner, smoothing out the rough edges of my life and making neat stacks of possibilities where there had once been impossible chaos. "I'm sure children thrive in this environment."

I knew my own would.

I loved my daughters more than life, but no matter how kind Brody or my sister tried to be about it, the truth was that I hadn't always been the best dad. Through Brody's encouragement, I felt closer to the girls than I ever had, but sometimes, it seemed like children ran on raw emotion, and I... well, I did *not*. Plus, I regularly got so caught up in work that I missed half of the girls' school events, playoff games, and awards ceremonies, even with Brody reminding me.

I would not let them miss out on this opportunity, too.

So I let my medical training take over, pushing out all peripheral distractions—like the truth—in pursuit of my objective.

"That sounds great," I lied. "We're... eager to get involved."

"Wonderful!" Dean Larson exclaimed. "Then I'd like to offer Jacey, Cleo, and Mia admission to Mountbatten Preparatory! School starts next Monday. We look forward to meeting your husband and introducing the two of you to all the other parents."

It wasn't until after I shook her hand, wrote her an appallingly large check, and went out to my car to call Brody with an update that I let the reality of the situation crash over me.

The girls could only attend if I had a *husband*...

And how the *fuck* was I going to find myself one of those in four days?

2

———————

BRODY

I ended the call with Grant—*Dr. Brighton*—and leaned over the table at the campus coffee shop table to bang my head repeatedly against my closed laptop. "*Moron.*"

"Wait, what? Are you talking about the admission people or Dr. Boss?" my friend Fen demanded, taking a seat on the opposite side of the table. She nudged a fresh cup of coffee in my direction. "What did I miss? Did the snooty school love the girls? Or are we toilet-papering houses?"

"Of course the school loved them. How could anyone not? Dr. Brighton said they're in." I sighed heavily. "It's me. I'm the moron. Always me."

"Aww." Fen ruffled my hair. "What's wrong, boo?"

I waved a hand. "The usual. I'm hopelessly in love with my boss. He's hopelessly oblivious."

"Ah. *That.*" She sighed. "What happened this time?"

I glanced up at her. "He sounded weird on the phone. He was calling from the car on his way from the school to the hospital, so maybe he was in work mode, but he didn't seem as excited as he should be. This is huge for the girls, you know? It almost felt like there was something he wasn't telling me. Sooo..." I winced. "I panicked. I was immediately convinced that Dr. Brighton had finally, four years in, apropos of nothing, noticed the giant, bulging heart-eyes I get whenever I'm around him and realized I had feelings for him—"

"Brody," she laughed, shaking her head. "Babydoll..."

"Yeah, I know. I'm ridiculous." I sat upright again. "But it gets worse. I started babbling about Gym Crush Dude. You know, the cute guy at my gym with the tattoos?"

She twisted her lips in thought and tilted her head until one of her two short pigtails was sticking straight up. "The one who's married? With children?"

"Right, but Grant—I mean, Dr. Brighton—doesn't know that. So I talked about how Gym Crush Dude was, like, *so* my type, with his muscles and blue eyes and tattoos—"

"Nooo," she moaned. "When he's the exact opposite of your actual type, which is brown-eyed, buttoned-up workaholics with adorable daughters?"

"Basically. And, like, Dr. Brighton knows I'm gay, but I have no idea how *he* identifies since he doesn't date—though he was in a relationship with a woman for long enough to have *three* children, so I'm guessing pretty straight—which means it's particularly mortifying that I started babbling about bulging biceps and dick prints—"

Fen gasped, but her eyes danced. "You did *not* mention Gym Crush Dude's dick print! What did Dr. Boss say?"

"He was horrified. I mean, he was really sweet and supportive and *perfect*, as usual. Like, 'Oh. That's... great for you, Brody. I hope things work out.' But there was this looooong awkward pause first, during which I died and only resuscitated myself because somebody needs to take Mia to dance this afternoon." I groaned and laid my forehead back on the computer. "How has he not fired me yet?"

"Because you're adorable. And the girls love you most. He couldn't run that household without you. Want more reasons?"

"No." I knew she was right, at least about the girls. "I just wish I didn't always come off as the clueless young college kid he thinks I am. When we're around the girls, everything is fine. I'm a normal person. He listens to me tell him about my classes, he vents to me about frustrations at work, he rolls his eyes to me about his sister, I talk about my friends. It's like an actual... friendship," I said at the last moment, because admitting that what I shared with my boss was basically the most satisfying relationship I'd ever had was just a little too pathetic. "But when we're alone, for some reason, I say the stupidest things. I wish I could talk to him and be..." I waved a hand, trying to grasp for the right words. "Interesting, worldly, fascinating—"

"Brody, sweetheart, *you are* interesting. You're amazing. No, stop," she said when I sat up and began shaking my head. She plucked my hand from the table and held it tightly in both of hers. "I'm serious. You've dealt with so many challenges—losing your parents and your brother in that accident, living on your own, putting yourself through college—"

"Fen, I love you, but that's not the same thing. Grant—*crap*. I need to stop slipping up, or I'm gonna end up calling him that to his face one of these days. *Dr. Brighton* is a freaking trauma surgeon. He goes to work every day and puts his hands inside people's bodies and puts them back together. He saves lives. He speaks fluent Spanish. He volunteers at a clinic downtown. He's just... a really good person."

"Yes, he's a nice guy, and yes, he does important work," she agreed, "but so do you—"

"His ex-wife just won an award for some photos she took of the floods in Australia that brought a lot of attention to the crisis," the throbbing bruise of jealousy in the center of my chest compelled me to add.

Fen huffed and let go of my hand to drink her coffee. "Liza also left town five years ago, and she only comes back for a week here and there to see her kids. Which is fine, that's her choice, and I'm sure she has many excellent qualities. But she's no saint, babydoll."

No, Liza wasn't a saint. I'd never actually met her, since Grant— fuck! *Dr. Brighton, Dr. Brighton, Dr. Brighton*—always gave me time off when she came to town, but as far as I was concerned, any woman who hadn't clung to a guy like him with both hands was suspect.

"Anyway." I pushed myself upright and sipped at my coffee before opening my laptop again. "I need to get back to work. Mia has jazz and ballet after camp, Cleo needs me to take her shopping, Dr. Brighton wants to talk to me tonight about 'expectations at Mountbatten,' whatever that means, and I have a project due in Probability and Statistics." I opened my file and shook my head. "I really hate this class. Tell me again why I saved it for my last semester?"

Fen tapped her lip with her pen. "Maybe because you have a problem where you put off stuff you know you're not going to enjoy?" she asked innocently.

My face heated. "My problem is that my best friend has taken too many psych classes and tries to analyze me."

Fen was undeterred. "Exhibit A: You have not told Dr. Boss that you are madly in love with him."

"My god." I shuddered at the very thought. "Never in a million years. Why the hell would I do that?"

"Because it's possible that he feels the same about you! No, I'm being serious." She shut my laptop screen when I attempted to ignore her. "You don't know his sexuality. For all you know, he's bi. Maybe he's fluid. You don't know everything there is to know about Dr. Boss's late-night love needs."

"Ew," I said, even though Grant's late-night love needs were a particular interest of mine.

"The man's a workaholic, Brody. But did you ever ask yourself why he throws himself into his work?"

"Uh, because he's damn good at it?" I shot back.

"Exactly," she approved. "Know what he's not good at? Figuring out emotional stuff. You know this. Just think of how hard it was for him to relate to the girls a couple years ago. How hard it *still* is for him sometimes. Maybe he needs to be reminded there's more to life than blood and guts in the emergency room."

I shook my head. "The man could be bi or pan or gay as fuck, and it doesn't mean he'd want anything to do with *me*, Fen. He's never made a single sexy eyeball in my direction, and believe me, I would have noticed. He's never even asked me to call him Grant." And that hurt. It was a sure sign he viewed me as an employee. Worse, as a kid.

"Okay, then." Fen studied me for a long moment while she sipped her drink. "Have you told him you're leaving?"

Oof.

"Kinda. Sorta." My stomach flipped over and landed with a sickening *thump*. "Okay, no. Not exactly," I admitted, though I heard Fen mentally tagging this as exhibit B in her Brody Doesn't Deal With Shit argument. "He knows I graduate at the end of this semester. *Finally.*"

"Brody. *My boo.* This is a man who forgets to eat dinner unless you remind him. You think he's put together 'Brody graduates' and 'Oh, shit, I need a new nanny'?"

"Full-time childcare specialist," I muttered, pulling my laptop open again.

"Babydoll, you need to that particular bull by the horns, for the girls' sake if not your own—"

"Shhhh! No talking." I said, putting a finger to my lips and nodding at my screen. "Busy. So busy. Probability. *Statistics.* Cannot be disturbed. Don't you have a class now?"

She sighed and grabbed her backpack, but before she left, she leaned toward me over the small table, impossible to ignore... though I tried. "I know you, Brody. You have a massive crush on this guy. You adore those girls. In some ways, it probably feels like you have a family back again, doesn't it? But babe, this is not real. And if you don't change *something* really soon—either shoot your shot or move on— you're gonna end up being his nanny for years, forgoing your own career... hell, forgoing all the loving, healthy *relationships* you could have. There's a good chance you're gonna end up miserable."

As she walked away, my phone dinged with an incoming text message, and my stupid heart beat out a crazy rhythm just seeing the name on my lock screen.

We. That single word made my stomach flip and my hands tremble. There was no *we*, though I'd do just about anything for a chance to make that happen.

As I stared out the door and across the sunny quad without really seeing any of it, I realized that I didn't need any skill in probabilities and statistics to know Fen was right.

~

For the rest of the school day, I tried desperately not to think about Gra—*Dr. Brighton.*

I failed.

When I finally left campus to pick up the girls from their last day of summer day camp and take them to their activities, they were chatty enough to distract me all the way up until dinner, but when Grant walked in the door carrying a stack of pizza and a weary smile, I was reminded all over again just how bad I had it for my straight employer.

"I'm home," he called, shutting the door to the garage with his foot.

I hurried over to take the pizza boxes out of his hands and set them on the kitchen table. "Good lord. Was Berlantis' having a sale?" I asked, laughing. "There's enough here for an army."

"I know." He blushed and ran a hand through his short brown hair before hanging his keys on the rack by the door next to mine. "But Jacey's decided to be a vegetarian, and Cleo loves pepperoni. And you like pesto, but Mia won't eat anything green, so I figured the easiest thing to do was to just get everyone their own." He tugged at the collar of his shirt and looked at me earnestly. "Was that not right?"

If the man knew how fucking close he was to having five foot nine inches of sexually frustrated childcare specialist attack him in his own home, he would not be so damn endearing without even warning a person.

"That's perfect," I assured him. "You remembered exactly right, Dr. Brighton. Thank you."

He nodded, clearly relieved, and I wanted so badly to kiss him I had to turn away and busy myself grabbing paper plates, napkins, and drinks for everyone.

This was the thing Fen got wrong in her armchair psychoanalysis —Grant wasn't bad at emotions. On the contrary. The man had a heart bigger than California, a mind like a steel trap, and a desperate desire to do right by everyone. Sometimes he just didn't seem to know how.

"You made good time," I said, keeping my eyes on the table as I set out the paper products. "That must mean the accident I heard about on the radio wasn't too bad."

He sighed and dropped his messenger bag on the counter. "No. And Dr. Osei was early for his shift, if you can believe it."

Mia came running into the kitchen and launched herself at her dad. "Daddy! My jazz class is having a recital at the end of summer. The song is 'Starlight' by Taylor Swift. You know that one about dancing? And *guess what*? I got a solo!"

Grant held her tight and squeezed his eyes closed in a way that did stupid shit to my heart. He truly did love his girls, even though his career demanded so much time away from them.

"That's amazing, peanut. Miss Jennie must think you're really talented."

"Jeannie," I corrected easily. "And Mia's been practicing really hard." I ruffled her hair.

Cleo came in and slumped in her chair at the table. "Are we going to eat? Because I'm starving, and Robbie stole my granola bar at lunch."

Mia struggled to get down from Grant's arms before calling Cleo on her lie. "Not true. You swapped with him for his crackers."

The girls squabbled for a moment for a moment about whether

crackers even counted as a snack while Grant watched the back-and-forth with the bewildered intensity of a chair umpire at Wimbledon. I turned away to call Jacey before my heart-eyes plopped out on the table.

Grant stepped behind me and lowered his voice. "You didn't tell them about Mountbatten?"

His warm breath hit the tender skin behind my ear, bringing up goose bumps all along my skin. I tried not to shiver. "Uh, no. Um... you said we... I mean, *you* would tell them."

He leaned over me to grab a piece of pesto pizza out of the box. "Thank you."

We moved to the table and settled in. Jacey took her seat next to Grant and eyed him with fourteen-year-old intensity. "Kinley said she saw you at Mountbatten today."

He nodded, fighting a smile. "Yup. I was there."

She huffed. "Did you... I mean... is there any, um, news?"

Grant tapped his chin. "News... hmm. What kind of news would I have gotten at Mountbatten? Perhaps I learned the Pythagorean theorem? Wait, that's not news. Pythagoras lived in 540 BC." He caught my eye across the table and winked, causing me to nearly aspirate my pizza.

"Dad," Jacey said, rolling her eyes. "Oh my god, your dad humor is soooo not funny. I'll literally *die* if we don't get in. Brody, please! Can't *you* make him tell us if—"

Grant smirked. "You're in."

The girls squealed with excitement, jumping up to hug him and thanking him profusely before turning to give me the same treatment.

"Hey, whoa. Don't thank me. I didn't do anything," I protested, returning their hugs.

"Not true," Grant said. "You filled out all the paperwork, you got the references, and you made sure I showed up on time."

"Brody always does *everything* to make us happy," Mia said as she settled back down to her pizza.

I smiled, but when I caught Grant's eye again, his grin had disappeared, and he was giving me a startled look like he'd never actually seen me before.

"What?" I demanded as the girls returned to their seats, chattering like a flock of excited magpies, and I pretended I didn't see Jacey breaking the no-phones-at-the-table rule to alert her friends. "Did I get something on me?" I reached out with my tongue to check that I didn't have pizza sauce on my lips.

Grant swallowed hard and looked away. "No. No, no. I was just... I need to talk to you after bedtime."

"Oh, right. About Mountbatten's expectations, you said?"

He nodded and toyed with the crust of his pizza.

I narrowed my eyes. "Is there a problem?"

He opened his mouth to answer when Mia jumped up. "Brody, can we do a dance party before bed? Please, please?"

Cleo rolled her eyes. "Brody doesn't get to pick the songs this time. He only ever plays Taylor Swift. *Borrring.*"

I clutched a hand to my chest. "You impertinent child. How dare you disrespect Taylor Swift at this dinner table."

She fought a smile. "Fine. You can pick, like, two songs. But not the *looooove* ones." She made a gagging noise. "Those are the worst."

"I'm well aware of your opinions on Taylor's catalog of romantic ballads," I said solemnly. "I would never."

Once they settled back down, Grant gave the girls more details. Their first day of school was in four short days, and orientation in two.

"Will you take us, Daddy?" Mia asked excitedly.

Grant winced. "I... I wish I could, peanut, but I'm scheduled to work those days. But Brody can take you, and you can tell me about it at dinner afterward, okay?"

Jacey looked up from her phone. "Dad, how many advanced classes did they say I can take? Cara says you need special permission to take more than three if you're involved in multiple extracurriculars. Did they say it was fine for me to take more?"

Grant blinked at her. "I... I'm sorry, sweetie. I didn't ask."

Her face fell. "You didn't *ask*? But Dad! That's, like, the whole *point* of me going to Mountbatten. I wanted access to the theater program *and* the academics."

"I... I didn't know. And the dean had some questions about..." Grant darted a guilty look in my direction, and his face flushed. "I was distracted."

"Typical," she said in a wounded, scathing tone. "Some patient was more important than your own kids, right? Leave it for the babysitter to handle?"

Grant's happy expression morphed into something halfway between annoyance and embarrassment. I could almost feel him shutting down. Still, he said sternly, "Be mad at me if you need to be, but don't be rude to Brody. He's more than just your babysitter, Jacey Louise."

"Jacey," I said abruptly. "We can get the permission you need later. And people forget important things all the time." I glanced pointedly at the phone that should not have been in her hands and lifted one eyebrow. "If someone is putting in serious effort to do the right thing, maybe you could give them the benefit of the doubt."

She set her phone facedown by her plate guiltily. "You're right. Sorry, Dad. And sorry, Brody. You know I love you, right?"

I nodded, and the conversation got back on track after that, with Cleo gabbing about Robotics Club at Mountbatten, while Mia gave a play-by-play of her dance class, Jacey added a few comments about her first year as a counselor-in-training, and I did an impression of my Technology in Society professor that got everyone laughing. Grant settled in, too, quietly cataloging and digesting facts while he ate his pizza.

Despite Grant's busy job at the hospital, he'd always made family dinner a priority. There were times he'd even come home for dinner just to turn around and leave again once the meal was over. It was the kind of attention and focus I'd missed after losing my own parents, and I loved him for giving it to his girls. He tried so hard to be a good dad.

As much as I wanted to ignore everything Fen had said earlier, she'd gotten one part right: this was exactly the life I'd dreamed of.

Sitting at a table, surrounded by the people I loved best in the whole world, feeling like an essential part of something.

It was really, *really* tempting to cling to a life that wasn't actually mine.

"Everything okay?" Grant murmured when the girls got up to clear the table. His kind eyes made the hair on my arms prickle.

"Yeah. Totally. Great." I swallowed. "Why wouldn't it be?"

A wrinkle appeared between his eyebrows, like he was trying to catalog my symptoms to make a diagnosis. It should not have been charming.

"Seriously, G—*Dr. Brighton*," I lied. I forced a big smile. "You ready for our dance party?"

He shook his head. "I don't, ah... No. You know I'm not a dancer. I'll clean up the kitchen. But after, when the girls are in bed, could you come to my office?"

I'd be lying if I said those words didn't conjure up a fantasy. One where Grant and I were a couple and he'd say those words to me with less confusion and more laughing innuendo. One where the night promised to end with him giving me a *thorough examination.*

Never happening, Kelly. Mind on your job.

But it was difficult to keep my mind there when the fantasy was so alluring. Later, when Mia, Cleo, and I were jumping around the living room to "Shake It Off" and even Jacey had deigned to sit on the sofa and lip-sync along with us, I noticed Grant leaning against his office doorframe with his ankles crossed, watching us from across the hall, and I couldn't help giving my ass a little extra shake, just in case. But when I turned back again a moment later, he was gone.

Jacey helped me get the younger girls ready for bed, and when they went down to say good night to Grant, she and I spent a couple of minutes talking about orientation and her idea of maybe switching from soccer to the cycling team at school this fall... which, she assured me with a blush, had *nothing* to do with Nolan Pettiwick, the boy who'd asked her to go mountain biking on Culpepper Trails, also being captain of Mountbatten's cycling team.

Oh, girl, I wanted to tell her. *Do not change your plans for a boy, no matter how cute he is...* but I wasn't that much of a hypocrite.

As I walked slowly back down to Grant's office, shutting out lights as I went, I thought about how much I loved the Brightons and how badly I wished I could be one of them somehow, never dreaming that I was about to be offered my chance...

And that I really should have been more specific about what I wished for.

3

GRANT

"You let her think *what*?" Brody demanded. His green eyes were sparkling but not with his usual laughter, and his dark hair stood on end from where he'd run his fingers through it repeatedly.

I wanted to reach out and tidy those strands, but I couldn't. For one thing, Brody was busy pacing the width of the small room, several feet away from where I was propped against my desk. For another, my hands had been shaking since the moment he'd walked into my office in his worn pajama pants and tight, faded unicorn T-shirt... and I had no idea how to make them stop.

I was a trauma surgeon, for god's sake. My hands *never* shook.

Then again, this situation was unprecedented on many levels, so maybe it shouldn't have been such a surprise.

"That I was married," I repeated, hoping I sounded calm. "To... you."

"But..." Brody paced to the wall and turned, barely flicking a glance in my direction. "But *why*?"

I frowned at him in concern. I knew he was overwhelmed by the news. Of course he was. But I'd already explained all this, I thought.

You probably could have found a better way to ease him into it rather than blurting out the whole truth, I chastised myself. *A scalpel instead of a hammer.* But it was too late to turn back now.

"As I said, the dean indicated that they require a certain level of family involvement, and full-time childcare professionals don't count. Since Liza's not here, and I'm so busy being the 'leading trauma surgeon in the state' or whatever you put on the application—"

"Don't you dare insinuate that this was my fault!"

"I'm not," I assured him quickly. "I'm not. But the fact of the matter is that, under the circumstances, I had to have a spouse, or the girls wouldn't have been able to attend Mountbatten."

"I get that part. I mean, I don't *get it* get it, because that policy is insane-o ridiculous, and I'm going to write a strongly worded letter to the dean, but..." Brody paused in by of one of the bookcases that lined the front of the room and turned to face me. "But why *me*?"

My brain blanked, and I stared back at him.

There were many solid answers to this. *The dean made a mistake, and I ran with it.* Or *There's no one I trust more with the girls.*

But the deeper truth was there was no one else it *could* be.

No one but Brody Kelly.

On any level.

Practically speaking, I didn't have any potential romantic prospects, let alone one who might pretend to be my spouse. I'd come out as gay five years ago, but in the intervening time, I hadn't had so much as a repeat sexual encounter, let alone anything approaching a relationship. It wasn't that I didn't want one, per se—I'd liked a lot of things about being in a relationship. I liked coming home to someone I could talk to and learn from. I liked having someone to focus on and make happy. I even liked engaging in comfortable, regular relation-ship sex, which might not be wildly innovative or exciting but left me feeling closer to my partner. I liked it all so much I'd stayed with Liza for years, even though things had started to get dicey long before Mia was born.

But when Liza had left me with a peck on the cheek, a stack of signed divorce papers, and three girls I felt unequipped to care for on my own, I'd had to admit the truth to myself: no matter how much I enjoyed being in a relationship, I simply... wasn't very good at it. I was too focused on work, with barely enough time to be a good dad, let alone a good partner.

Besides which, for the past four years, I'd had... Brody.

We were not in a relationship—god, no—which was why he'd put up with me as long as he had. But he was so... *there*—a constant, sunshiny presence in my life, whether he was talking to me about his classes and his friends, or flailing his arms and twirling around the living room to Taylor Swift at top volume, or helping me decide how young was too young for a teenager to have a cell phone—that it *almost* didn't matter that we weren't officially together or that I was the exact opposite of the guys he wanted sexually.

Sex was overrated, really. And sex with Brody, no matter how compelling he was, would be—

I swallowed hard, and the vision popped into my brain of me, stalking across the floor and pressing Brody back into the bookcase. Of his green eyes widening with heat at the hardness of my body against his. Of his breaths coming shallow and fast. Of him smiling at me in welcome so I could press my tongue to that perfect dimple, lick the salt from his skin, and—*fuck*.

I moved my gaze to the carpet at Brody's feet and twisted my hips to hide my rapidly inflating cock.

Frontal bone, temporal bone.

Deflate, I told my dick sternly. *He is not for you.*

But my skin prickled, and my empty hands ached.

Sphenoid bone. Hyoid bone.

You're his boss, for god's sake. I gripped the edge of the desk behind me. *Stop being weird.*

Maxilla. Mandible.

"Gr—Dr. Brighton?" Brody pressed.

I darted a nervous glance up at him.

One of Brody's toned arms was wrapped around his stomach protectively, but the other was raised so that he could more efficiently tug at his hair. He looked so angry and... and *hurt*, maybe, that I wanted to haul him against my chest comfortingly and vow to protect him like a knight in shining armor.

Which was ridiculous, of course. Brody was the strongest person I knew, and I wasn't a person anyone turned to for comfort. Not to mention, I was the person who'd upset him in the first place.

"Are you okay?" Brody demanded, frowning at me worriedly, his anger temporarily on hold. "You look like you're going to throw up." He closed the distance between us, bringing his hand up to test the temperature of my forehead like I was one of the girls. "You do feel a little feverish."

I jerked my head away from his gentle, electrifying touch. "M'not feverish."

"Do you think it was the pizza?" He moved his hand to my cheek and then to cup the back of my neck, almost like he was pulling me in for a kiss, and I swear I could feel the tiny electrical charges jumping from synapse to synapse beneath his fingertips. "Because I feel fine, but I didn't try the pepperoni— "

"It's not the pepperoni," I groaned, suddenly, shockingly breathless.

"It could be an allergic reaction. Do your lips feel tingly?" He brushed his fingers over them lightly, and damn if they didn't *start* tingling right then.

I licked them instinctively, right over the place he'd touched, and every muscle in my body locked. "Brody—"

"You're breathing funny," he pronounced. "That's it. I'm calling an ambulance. I know you're a doctor, but there's a reason everyone says doctors make the worst patients." He started to move away like he was going to find his phone.

With a speed and strength I didn't know I possessed, I grabbed his wrist before he could take a single step.

"I'm not sick," I said roughly.

Brody froze, his gaze pinging from my face to my hand, where it was clamped around his. "Dr. Brighton..."

"Grant," I corrected in a whisper, aching to hear my name on his lips so badly that I couldn't remember any of the very compelling reasons why it had been important to maintain that formality, to put distance between us.

Like the fact that he was ten years younger than me.

Or that I was not the kind of guy he wanted.

Or that I *paid his salary.*

Fuck.

I sidestepped away from him and turned toward the darkened window that overlooked the side of the house, pretending to be fascinated by the view, though I could see nothing but the reflection of my own pained, hungry expression... and Brody's wide-eyed, confused one.

Humerus. Scapula. Clavicle.

"Sorry," I managed once I was able to squeeze words out in some semblance of a normal voice. "I just meant that, ah... under the circumstances, you should call me Grant. If you want. Not a big deal, either way." I forced a laugh.

"Are you... are you sure you're okay?" he asked slowly.

I nodded without turning around. "Upset at myself for causing this situation. For letting it get this far." That was the truth, at least. "The dean made assumptions when she saw your name as an emergency contact on the application, and I didn't correct her. I didn't know how. I'm sorry, Brody. I swear, I'm not trying to pressure you into lying for me o-or worse, marrying me."

I really *hadn't* imagined involving Brody in my lie at all... at least until halfway through dinner, when Brody had been so perfectly *Brody,* and Mia had made a comment about how dedicated he was to making the girls happy, and I'd looked at him across the table and thought, *Yes. Marry him. Keep him.*

Now I couldn't get the thought out of my mind.

He let out a strangled sound, and I wished that I could see his face, but I couldn't turn without showing off a very clear and present —what had he called it on the phone earlier?—dick print against my khaki slacks.

My dick, at least, did not feel that sex with Brody would be over-rated. Not in the slightest.

"Okay." Brody blew out a breath, and in my peripheral vision, I saw him begin pacing again. "Okay, let's think about this." It sounded like he was talking more to himself than to me, so I didn't interrupt. "You need a spouse. At least temporarily. And I don't suppose you've been, um... dating anyone you haven't mentioned?"

"No." I turned from the window and retreated behind my desk, desperately trying to gain back some distance... though the fact that his pajamas rode lower and lower on his lean hips as he paced was making that extremely difficult to achieve.

"Really? No one? Not, like, a nice—" He cleared his throat. "—woman that you maybe meet for, um, lunches or... anything?"

"No. There's no one," I admitted. "I haven't dated in years."

"Right. Good. I mean... *ha*. I mean, not *good*. But, um... good to *know*. For... for planning purposes." He nodded to himself. "And what about Liza? I know she's busy, but maybe she could come back—"

I shook my head before he could finish speaking. "When I spoke to her a couple of weeks ago, Liza was in Georgia—the country, not the state." At least, I was pretty sure that was the Georgia she meant. "And she hasn't even made it back for a visit since the girls' spring break last March. She loves them, but when she left, she made it clear that she was at the end of her 'full-time parenting era.' I can't imagine that she'd come back for this."

Brody grimaced. "Lovely. Okay. So... It's not the divorced thing that the school has a problem with, right?"

"That's my understanding. If Liza or I were around more, this wouldn't be an issue."

"But there must be all sorts of cases where parents can *plan* to get involved but can't for various reasons, like if they get ill, or have to take care of someone who is, or if they have a new baby. I can't imagine they'd make students leave if that happened."

I shrugged and nodded, not sure where he was going with this. "Probably not."

"So, really, you only need someone as a... a *temporary* spouse. For the first school year, let's say." Brody's eyes flashed in my direction, and he began speaking—and pacing—faster, like he was trying to convince me of something. Or maybe convince himself. "Someone who'll do what I'm already doing for the girls—managing their extracurriculars, chaperoning, and volunteering, that sort of thing."

My heart rate picked up again, and my stomach clenched as I imagined where he was going with this. Was he actually offering to —? Agreeing to—?

"Brody, would you—?"

Brody stopped short, then shut his eyes and bit his lip. "I'm leaving," he blurted.

I pushed to my feet in one jerky movement. "You what? Is it because of this? Because I'll tell the dean there was a mistake. The girls will understand—"

"No." He pushed both hands through his hair again. "No, I mean... I'm leaving at the end of the semester." He turned toward me with his feet braced apart like he was preparing to fight a battle. "I'm graduating in December, remember? And I need to find a job. A *software* job. So I can start saving up money—"

"To start your own company," I finished, falling back into my chair. My stomach clenched again for an entirely different reason. "We've talked about that so many times in the past, but I guess I didn't let myself think about how soon that would be happening. Well. Obviously, you won't have to move out until you're ready. You can live here indefinitely, even after—"

"No," Brody said in a strangled voice. "I really can't. I'll still see the girls as much as I can. As much as you'll let me. But you'll need the room." He gave me a lopsided smile. "For the new nanny."

"Full-time childcare specialist," I mused, my mind already shying away from contemplating a time when Brody wouldn't live here.

Instead, a new thought occurred to me. A solution to *both* of our problems. And I was steadfastly ignoring all the warning bells going off in my head as to why it was an absolutely terrible idea.

Brody laughed. "Nah. The new person won't get to call themselves that until I've given my stamp of approval," he teased. But his smile fell away quickly. "Anyway, all of that is to say I don't think I can be a solution to this problem—"

"But you could," I disagreed quickly. "I… I have an idea that might work, if you agree to it."

He frowned. "I'm listening."

"What if…" I began. Then I hesitated.

This setup was all wrong. He was standing too far away, and our positions reminded me of the day I'd hired him, four years ago. He'd stepped into this very office that day wearing a fitted button-down and ripped jeans that made him look so damn young—and light-years less qualified than the professional nannies I'd already interviewed for the position—that if he hadn't been so eager and convincing, I never would have hired him.

But Brody wasn't a job candidate now. In a strange way, *I* was.

I stood up again and came around the desk, herding him toward the small sofa opposite the window.

"Okay, you're scaring me a little. What's your idea?" he demanded when he'd taken a seat beside me.

I turned toward him. My knee brushed his, and I pretended I couldn't feel the heat of him through two layers of fabric… and that it wasn't eliciting a predictable biological response in certain already overstimulated areas of my body. "What if I supported you so you could start your own company?"

His sharp green gaze ping-ponged around my face. "Supported me."

"Yes!" I tugged at my shirt collar. *Be convincing, Grant.* "After you graduate, you could start your company here and work from home while the girls are at school. I could continue to pay your salary. You could keep volunteering and managing their activities like you do now. You could save up money since you won't have tuition to pay or room and board. Everything could stay the same." I swallowed nervously before adding, "We could even get married for real. O-on paper, I mean. Then you'd qualify for benefits on my plan at work."

Brody stared at me. I could feel the excitement and nerves jangling in the air between us. This was either the stupidest idea I'd ever had or the most brilliant.

"I, ah…" He opened his mouth, then shut it again.

"Yes?" I leaned forward eagerly.

"I'm concerned that, um..."

"Go on."

"You... you do realize I'm a *man*," he blurted.

I blinked at him. Of all the things I'd expected him to say, all the many objections I'd expected him to come up with, that one hadn't entered my mind. But he seemed... agitated about it, for some reason, so I kept my face neutral. "That hadn't escaped my notice," I said gravely.

Brody huffed. "I mean, if you married a man, people would assume you're gay."

"Right." I still wasn't sure what the problem was, and I felt a little foolish. I needed Gwen here to help me see what emotional context I was missing. Hell, I needed Brody himself. "The dean already thinks that since she assumed you were my husband," I pointed out.

"And that's not a problem for you?"

"Uh. Well. No? Since I *am* gay—"

"You're *gay*?" Brody jumped up and began pacing again. His voice was so comically high-pitched I almost laughed, but something told me he wouldn't appreciate that. "Why haven't you ever said so? Not that you needed to tell me or anyone, obviously, but... *why didn't you tell me?*"

"I suppose because, um..." I swallowed. I hadn't told him for the same reason I'd never encouraged him to talk about men he dated. Because it would make it that much harder for me to keep things professional. "...it never came up?"

Brody shook his head wordlessly.

"I didn't fully realize it until a few years ago," I offered, leaning forward to rest my elbows on my knees and keeping my gaze trained on the carpet. "When I was younger, I was focused on school and didn't actually want to date anyone. And then Liza and I met in college, and after that, things just sort of... happened, I guess. She got pregnant with Jacey, so we got married. I was busy with medical school, then building my career, while Liza seemed happy doing part-time photography and being with the kids. Looking back, it was easier for both of us to just keep going with the flow without thinking too hard. But then Liza finally admitted she *wasn't* happy, and we saw a marriage counselor who encouraged us to explore our passions individually." I shrugged. "It turned out Liza had never wanted... this." I waved a hand to indicate my big house in its tree-lined subdivision, as well as the three children tucked in their beds... and myself. "And that I was more attracted to men... and maybe always had been."

I darted a glance up at Brody, who was staring at me in shock, and quickly looked away, feeling my cheeks go hot with embarrassment. *Who doesn't know something so essential about themselves until they're thirty?*

"That must've been overwhelming as fuck," Brody murmured sympathetically. He sat back down beside me. "Like a bomb went off in the middle of your life, making you question *everything*."

I stared at him mutely. I'd never met anyone else who understood that. Even Gwen, who'd never liked Liza, had assumed I'd feel relieved and *free* that I could truly be myself, but I hadn't. I liked order and clarity, and the dissolution of my marriage had brought chaos.

Of course, it had also brought Brody, so it wasn't all bad.

"Did you... date?" he asked gently.

I rolled my eyes and laughed a little. "Oh yeah. For a few months there, I dated nonstop. You do remember Gwen is my sister, right? She pushed me to get out and meet people... and she was right, in a way. I learned a lot very quickly."

For one thing, I'd learned that I was definitely gay... and for another, that casual sex was not for me, for a variety of reasons.

"Oh." Brody folded his hands in his lap, almost... disappointed. "It's weird. I'm trying to picture you dancing down at the Cathedral on a Friday night..."

"Is that the Shirtless Men Drink Free night?" I wondered.

He nodded.

Strangely, I was having no trouble picturing *Brody* shirtless in a pack of closely pressed bodies—a sexier but equally joyful version of him dancing in the living room to Taylor Swift. I could also easily imagine every man in the place wanting to take him to bed, too.

Christ, pretending to be married to him is going to be torture. I tugged at my shirt collar, which had grown impossibly tight for some reason.

"Do you have someone?" I demanded suddenly. "I mean, I know you and Milo broke up a while ago—"

"Entitled ass," Brody muttered, echoing my own jealous thoughts.

"—but if you're seeing someone you haven't mentioned, like that guy at your gym—"

"No," he said quickly, shaking his head. "There's only... I mean... no."

A blush streaked down his neck, and I wondered if the skin there would feel warm against my tongue. I squeezed my eyes closed to block out the gorgeous sight of him. "Good," I said in a strangled voice. "That makes things more straightforward."

"I guess. But what about the girls?" Brody's eyes searched mine. "What do we tell them?"

"I don't know." It should have been a red flag, how quickly I was pushing this idea forward when so many questions remained unanswered. It wasn't like me. But I had no desire to slow things down or to rethink. Especially not after Brody had reminded me that he would be graduating—potentially *leaving*—in just a matter of months. "I suppose it would be easier not to tell them anything? I can tell the dean that we don't refer to you as a step-parent. You're just... Brody."

Brody nodded. "We *could* tell them the truth, but the younger girls would have trouble keeping the secret. Jacey might, too. It's a lot to put on them. They might wonder if it was... real." His blush deepened.

"Besides, the marriage will be nothing more than paperwork," I said firmly, praying that my own dick would get the message. "A change to your employment contract. Everything else in our lives will stay the same, so there's no need to confuse them. Right?"

"Right," Brody agreed just as firmly, sticking out his hand for me to shake. "Nothing will change, and no one will ever know."

I was pretty sure we both knew we were deluding ourselves about how easy it would be, since it felt like a Gordion knot of lies already, but as I clasped his warm palm in mine, I decided that it didn't matter. Brody and I would take things as they came.

But we had no idea how quickly it would all unravel.

4

BRODY

I should have known something was up the minute I got the kids to the neighborhood pool for the end-of-summer party.

It had been three days since Grant and I shook hands on our deal. Two days since we'd snuck down to city hall on his lunch break, gotten married by a justice of the peace, and celebrated by toasting with ice cream cones after taking the girls for a walk in the park. One day since I'd successfully navigated Mountbatten's intensive orientation program with a freshman, a fifth grader, and a first grader. Twelve measly hours since I'd waved good night to *my husband* at the top of the stairs and assured him, "I really think this is going to work. No one's going to know," before retreating to my bed and jerking myself off to the memory of him saying, "I take thee, Brody..."

Past me had been criminally naive and foolish.

But I'd no sooner topped off the girls with fresh sunscreen, set them loose to find their friends, and laid out my towel on a chaise lounge in the shade than I was surrounded by a group of self-tanned and highlighted neighborhood hyenas who smelled fresh blood. Namely, *mine.*

"Brody." Margot Jennings, whose son was Cleo's age, settled

herself sideways on the lounge chair to my left and looked at me over the top of her designer sunglasses. "I'm not mad, I'm disappointed."

"Okay?" I pulled my water bottle out of my giant cooler bag and leaned back in my chair. "What happened? Is it the class schedules? Did Oliver get Mr. Bennet for Algebra I?"

"They haven't released the schedules yet." Candace Bowen, whose daughter was a year older than Mia, plopped herself down by my feet and proceeded to breastfeed Teddy, her youngest, effectively blocking me in. "This disappointment is *personal.*"

"Er..." I fiddled with my sunglasses and pulled my hat down lower. *Calm down,* I told myself. *Nobody saw us at the courthouse. The marriage certificate hasn't even been filed yet. They can't possibly know unless—*

"My housekeeper's sister works at the records office at city hall," Meera Dewan said conversationally, pulling the chair on my right so close that I could smell the Tom Ford Soleil Blanc wafting off her. "She saw two hot dudes getting married the other day, and one was Dr. Brighton, the surgeon who took out her appendix. She said he was robbing the cradle. Would you know anything about that?"

"What?" I laughed uneasily. "No. That's. *Heh.* I mean. Lots of people look like other people, Meera—"

"True." Paul Norris, whose twins were Jacey's age, parked himself beside Margot. "Which is why, when Meera mentioned it to me, I asked Roberta Allen if she'd heard anything. Roberta's wife volunteers in the admin office at Mountbatten." He lifted one eyebrow. "She said Grant's *husband* is listed as the girls' second emergency contact."

"I..." I felt my face going red.

"Holy shi... shiitake mushrooms," Candace breathed with a guilty glance down at her toddler. "I knew it! I told Max at breakfast, and he was all, 'No way. Grant Brighton's straight. And even if he weren't, he'd never fool around with his *nanny*—'"

"Full-time childcare specialist," I muttered. "And Max is right. Grant wouldn't. He didn't! It wasn't like that. See, what happened was..." I trailed off.

Shit.

What happened was Grant and I were a pair of idiots who'd spent so much time congratulating ourselves on keeping a secret that we hadn't come up with a plan for what to do if we got found out.

"You got married without inviting us," Margot said unhappily. "We didn't even get to give you a bachelor party. Or a shower. I throw the *best* showers."

"It was a very quiet event," I said desperately. "A small, spontaneous little..." I cleared my throat. "...marriage. Just me and Grant. We haven't even told the girls yet. They're dealing with so much already, changing schools, and we want to, you know, make sure things are as stable as possible for them—"

"Why in the world would you worry about that?" Meera demanded. "The girls love you. They'll be thrilled. Besides, some of us have known for a while that Grant wasn't straight."

Candace nodded. "I told Max that, too."

"Anyone with *eyes* could see the way you've looked at each other for years. Like he's the sun you revolve around and you're the stars that guide him, or so Javier tells me," Paul said with an eye roll for his poetic husband. "It's *nauseating*, FYI, and sets the bar way too high for the rest of us."

"No." I shook my head frantically. "That's not true."

"Don't bother denying it. There's no way you're going to keep this a secret. Roberta's chatty," Margot said with a disapproving look, as though she wasn't the unofficial head of the neighborhood gossip network. "And this story is way too cute to keep quiet. Besides, it's not like you committed a murder. You fell in love."

"Yeah, I guess I did," I sighed. I couldn't bring myself to deny it. "But it's complicated, okay. Grant and I—"

"Awww. You're already talking like a couple! Are you going to be a Brighton now that you're married?" Meera asked eagerly. "Grant and Brody Brighton sounds so adorab— *Oh.*"

Candace glanced up, and her gaze caught at something over my shoulder. Paul looked, too, and he winced. A sick feeling swelled in my gut even before a small voice from behind me said, "Brody?"

I turned around to find Jacey standing by my chair. "I came back for my goggles," she whispered, darting a glance at the assembled adults that made it clear she'd overheard at least some part of the discussion.

"Oh, sweetheart." I reached for her, but she took a step back. "Hang on. Let me explain."

"Is it true? You and Dad... got *married*?" Her face held a combination of hope and fear, but I wasn't sure which outcome she hoped for and which she feared.

I hesitated... and that was all the answer she needed. She jerked out of my reach and bolted toward the ladies' room.

Shit.

"Brody, we're so sorry. We didn't see her," Margot began, but I didn't stop to reassure her or explain.

"Watch the girls, please!" I yelled, and then I hurled myself off the side of the chaise, only pausing to grab my phone, and ran after Jacey, who was heading for the clubhouse.

When she disappeared inside the women's changing room, I dialed Grant.

"Dr. Brighton," he said in his clipped work tone.

Thank god.

"Everyone's okay. We're fine," I reassured him first. I'd learned the hard way that a call from me in the middle of the day gave him an immediate surge of adrenaline because, as a trauma surgeon, he assumed the worst. "But there's a problem with our, uh... secret." I glanced around and lowered my voice further. "The neighborhood parents found out that we got married, and when they asked me about it, Jacey overheard and ran off. She seemed upset."

"*Fuck.*"

My heart leaped up into my throat. Grant rarely cursed in public, and he sure as hell didn't at work. "I'm sorry," I blurted, as if I'd splashed it all over social media.

"Not your fault, Brody." His voice was filled with regret. "It was naive of me to think we could keep it a secret. This was my doing."

"*Our* doing," I corrected. "I agreed to it. Don't forget that."

"No," he whispered, low and intimate. "I haven't forgotten."

I knew, logically, that he was only lowering his voice so he wouldn't be overheard at work, but my stupid heart couldn't help interpreting his tone in a different way—a way that made logic fly out the window, just as it had the other night when I'd agreed to this scheme.

There were a billion reasons why marrying Grant was the most ridiculous thing I'd ever done and bound to end in disaster—Fen had laid out every single one to me in scathing detail when I'd told her about this yesterday—but the most important by far was that we'd created a situation where the girls could get hurt... and now one of them *had*.

I should have seen this coming a mile off, and my own ceaseless *wanting* had made me blind to it.

"She ran into the changing room," I told him. "I'm going to try to talk to her when she comes out. To explain. I'm going to tell her the truth. Unless... do you want to tell her yourself?"

"No. You know I trust you." Grant blew out a breath. "Please tell her why we did it and why we kept it quiet. And I suppose I can look into getting an annulment and finding the girls another school, if it comes to that."

"If we have to," I hedged. "But that's a last resort. I think Jacey will understand once I explain that we did it for the girls."

I could almost hear Fen's laughing voice from last night, as though she was standing here with me. *Oh, sure. You did it for the girls. It has nothing at all to do with your need to cling to the Brighton kids and their father for as long as you can, right?*

"I hope so. I don't want Jacey to be upset at you when you're only trying to help her." Grant took a breath. I could picture his long fingers threading through his hair. "I'm sorry, Brody. I should have asked. Are *you* okay?"

His kindness caught me off guard, and tears filled my eyes.

No. No, I'm not. I'm calling you Grant in my head all the time now, even though I haven't said it out loud. I'm finding it even harder to keep my distance. Jacey's upset, and I'm afraid I'm going to get my heart broken, and it's still not real... *and I should really regret marrying you more than I do.*

"You don't need to worry about me," I said softly.

"But I do." Grant's voice was hard to make out over the sound of the hospital's intercom system paging people. Any minute, he'd be called away to get back to work. "We'll figure this out, okay? We'll do whatever we have to do. If you need me to leave early, I'll—" A commotion came over the line, and I heard Grant bark that he'd be right there. "Shit. Brody, I've got to go. But call me again if you need me. And I promise, no matter what happens, I'll make sure you're taken care of. Okay?"

I shut my eyes. God, I wished he meant that in a way that had nothing to do with money and contracts.

"Yeah," I whispered. "I'll let you know how it goes. Maybe Jacey will have an idea we haven't thought of. She's brilliant, even if she's only fourteen."

Grant blew out a harried breath. "Yeah. Let me know. And please, tell Jacey I love her."

"I will." Jacey peeked out of the ladies' room as if determining whether she was clear to come out. I lifted my eyebrows at her. "Later," I murmured into the phone before ending the call. "Jacey, come talk to me for a minute?"

She looked ready to argue.

"Please, sweetheart?" I begged. "Let me explain."

She emerged cautiously and took a seat in the upholstered chair I indicated in a small alcove. She looked equal parts angry and hurt.

"Okay, first... I'm so sorry you overheard that conversation. I didn't want you to find out that way."

"It sounds like you didn't want me to find out *at all,*" she shot back. "How could you get married without telling us? Oh, my god. Like, who even does that? Was this Dad's idea?"

"We didn't..." The denial stuck in my throat, and I broke off, rubbing a hand over my head in frustration. "It's complicated."

"Then explain it! I'm not a little *kid,* Brody. I'm *fourteen.* God! Is it that Dad thinks I don't know he's gay? Because I do, and I don't give a shit! Half my friends are queer or questioning. So he's gay. *Who cares?*"

"Language," I said sharply. Her expression turned mutinous. "I'm serious, Jace. I'm about to explain a very confidential situation to you. Please show me that you're mature enough to know when and how you can use your words, okay?"

She nodded once and sat up straighter in her seat, trying so hard to project *adult* that my heart squeezed with affection. There was really nothing I wouldn't do for this girl or her sisters.

"Okay. When your dad met with the dean of admissions at Mountbatten, she explained that the school had an unofficial two-parent policy."

"A... what?" she demanded. "That's ridiculous! So, like, people can't be divorced? What is this, the 1900s?"

I winced. "Please remember some of us were born way back in the 1900s, m'kay? But I don't disagree with you. It's a ridiculous policy. It's not that people can't be divorced, exactly, but they do require families to devote a certain amount of time to the school or whatever. It's part of their school culture. And I agree that it's a good idea in theory, but—"

"But there are single parents who don't have time to do that stuff. Single parents who are working three jobs or whatever—"

"Exactly." I nodded. "Or in your case, a single parent who's working one very demanding job." She rolled her eyes, but I pressed her on it. "Your dad makes a lot of money, Jacey, but he works just as hard as any other single parent who's trying to support a household. He's just fortunate enough to have the money to pay someone to help out."

"I guess," she allowed.

"Your dad loves you girls more than anything. And that's why, when the dean made the assumption that I was your dad's *husband* instead of his employee, your dad went along with it. Because he knows how badly you want to attend Mountbatten."

"Oh my god. Really? He did that for us?" She blinked. "Wait, but he didn't even talk to you about it first?"

I shook my head. "He couldn't. Not in the moment. He talked to me about it the other night. After pizza. And I... I agreed that we should get married *on paper*. It's not a real marriage, with... dating o- or *feelings*. It's more like a business arrangement. A temporary thing. And in the meantime, I get to be on his health insurance at work, and I'll stay here for a while after I graduate in December so I can save up to start my own business."

Jacey nodded, though she still looked troubled. "The app that you're making."

"Right. This way, I don't have to get a full-time job and pay for rent somewhere else. I'll get to be with you guys while I'm saving up." I shrugged. "It's not something we ever would have considered if it weren't for the school's policy, but it seemed like a decent plan. We planned to keep it all private. Not a lie, just... not sharing that things had changed behind the scenes." I grimaced. The rationalization sounded lame coming out of my own mouth, and Jacey was way too smart not to call me on it. I hurried to add, "But it looks like that's not going to be possible. A lot of the parents figured it out. People love gossip."

She tilted her head to one side. "More like people love *you*. And Dad, obviously. But, like, they want to know because they care."

Huh. "I guess that's true," I allowed.

She stared down at her fingernails, where last week's bright nail colors were chipped and mangled. "So... now what are you going to do?"

"Well... part of that depends on you, I guess. It was one thing for us not to tell people about the marriage, but it's another thing for people to know we're married and for us to have to pretend to be a couple when we're in public. That *would* be lying. And now that you know, you'll have to keep that secret, too, which isn't a position your dad or I wanted you to be in. The alternative, though, is to come clean and find a new school. What do you think?"

Jacey studied me for a long moment, defiant and hopeful at the same time, and I could almost see her brain churning as she tried to come up with a solution. "Do you like him?" she blurted finally.

I frowned. "Your dad? Of course I like him. He's wonderful." Then the true meaning of her question hit me. "Oh! Do I *like him* like him. I... well. I didn't even realize he was gay until three days ago, Jace." Not that I'd let that stop me from fantasizing. A lot.

Her eyes narrowed. "That's not an answer," she pointed out. "Because if you do like him, Brody, maybe you could try it. Just for a while. Just to see. You're both gay, and you both care about each other. You're young, and you're cute. Sorta."

"Stop. You'll make me blush," I said wryly.

Jacey laughed. "And Dad's old and boring, but not, like, *really* gross-looking, right? He's smart and successful, and his jokes aren't *always* cheesy. And he makes good pancakes. And I know it's annoying that he leaves his dirty cream cheese knife on the edge of the sink like he's going to make another bagel—which he never does —and he leaves empty water bottles rolling around in his car all the time, and he works way too much, but he always listens when you talk to him about that stuff, Brody. So maybe you could *try* to like him that way."

I laughed weakly. She had no idea. None.

"'Cause if you *did* like each other," she said softly, "then it wouldn't really matter how your relationship started. It would be real, and no one would be lying at all." She swallowed. "And then, you'd stay with us always."

"Oh, sweetheart." Impulsively, I grabbed her hand. "I've told you —it doesn't matter if I work for your dad or not, you and your sisters are always going to be my special girls. Your dad would have to barricade the door to get me to stop seeing you—"

"I know. But it won't be the same, will it?"

I opened my mouth, then closed it again. It wouldn't, and I couldn't pretend otherwise.

Jacey shrugged, then nodded resolutely, pulling her hand away. "Okay, so if you're asking for my opinion or what I feel comfortable saying, I wanna tell everyone you're married. Cleo, Mia, Aunt Gwen... everyone. I wanna say, 'My dad and Brody are husbands now, and Cleo, Mia, and I are really hoping it'll work out for those crazy lovebirds.' I want to wish it so hard it comes true. Because if it doesn't work out, Brody," she added gently, "it's not gonna hurt more when you leave because you're *divorcing* than it would if you were leaving because you got another job. Me and Cleo and Mia already handled our parents' divorce, remember?"

"Yeah. I do."

"And Mom already got remarried and divorced again, and we handled that, too. It wasn't the same because we only knew Elias for maybe three weeks of that time—remember when they took us to New Zealand on the *Lord of the Rings* tour a few years ago?"

"I remember," I agreed.

I remembered Grant complaining about the girls going on a tour of a movie they'd been too young to even watch. I remembered he'd spent the three weeks of their trip working extra hours at the hospital just to keep himself distracted. And I remembered that when he *had* come home, he'd fallen asleep on the sofa with the TV playing old Doris Day movies, and I'd covered him with a blanket while wishing desperately he'd make a move on me while the girls were out of the country... but he hadn't, damn it.

Even after all this time, even after getting freaking *married*, he hadn't.

Which meant he *wouldn't*. He might be it for me, but I wasn't it for him. Deluding myself that this arrangement would have a happily ever after was about as effective as Jacey "wishing it true."

"The point is, it's the *losing you* part that'll hurt, Brody, not the divorce part."

Her words made me feel both better and worse. It helped to know the marriage bargain wasn't going to make things worse for them, but knowing that eventually I'd have to leave—because, as Fen said, "*every fairy tale has to end sometime, boo*"—killed me as much as it did her.

"Have I mentioned today how very smart you are?" I asked roughly. "Because you are, Jacey Brighton. You're absolutely brilliant. And I could not love you more."

To my shock, her eyes welled with tears. "Back atcha. You're like a dad... only cooler." She sniffed and assumed her usual disdainful teenager expression to cover it. "Like, a *tiny* bit cooler."

Oh, my fucking heart.

"It's my musical taste that gets me the cool points, isn't it?" I joked, nudging her arm. "Should I break into some 'Exile'? You can sing the Taylor parts."

She rolled her eyes but giggled, just as I'd known she would. "I lied. You're not cooler. Not even a little cooler."

I laughed, too. Then I looked out the clubhouse door at the late-summer sunshine, where my friends and her sisters waited. "What do you say we go home?" I asked abruptly. "We can get strawberry lemonade slushies on the way and do a backyard dance party this time..."

"And you can figure out how you and Dad should tell Mia and Cleo about being married before Mrs. Dewan spills the beans?" she asked shrewdly. "I vote yes. But," she added in a judgmental Cleo-voice, "no *love songs* at the dance party."

I chuckled and made a cross over my heart. "I would never."

I stood and grabbed her hand to help pull her to her feet, but she shocked me by throwing her arms around me and hugging me tightly. "Just don't leave us, okay? Even if you and Dad have to split up someday, don't leave like Mom did. That's the only thing you could do that would..."

The words *that would break* us remained unspoken.

I leaned over and pressed a kiss to her forehead. "I will never walk away from you. That's something I can definitely promise."

And I meant those words with every part of myself—nothing in the world could make me stop loving these girls.

But I was very afraid they were equally true for their father.

5

GRANT

Three weeks into the school year, I found myself standing on the sidelines, toying with the shiny platinum ring on my finger as I watched Brody set up drinks and snacks on a picnic blanket with the other soccer parents, and I wondered how my busy, structured life had suddenly veered into... *this*.

A life where I was spending my Saturday morning standing outside, on a field, in the September sunshine.

A life where my daughters were also voluntarily awake and outside, happily talking and laughing with their friends, despite the early hour, as though adjusting to their new school—and new stepdad—had been easy peasy.

A life where I was...

"*Married*." My sister, Gwen, stood beside me in her Mountbatten sweatshirt, and for a startled second, I thought she'd read my mind. But then I saw that she'd followed the direction of my gaze and was watching Brody also, with a face full of fond affection. "Fucking *married*."

"I told you this weeks ago," I muttered under my breath. "Yet every time I see you, you say it like you're shocked all over again."

"Because it *is* a shock," she said with a laugh. "I still can't believe that my brother—buttoned-up, oh-so-reserved Dr. Grant Brighton—married his *nanny*. His *male* nanny. It's the scandal of the century. Just ask the ladies in Mom's mahjong club."

"I really wish you hadn't told Mom quite the way you did. She thinks it's..." I darted a covert glance around the Mountbatten soccer field before saying in a whisper. "...*real.*"

"Dude. Shiny hardware you two have on your fingers suggests it's very real." She elbowed me lightly. "So does the marriage certificate."

I rolled my eyes. "Yes, but there are special circumstances, as you know."

"Oh, I know the circumstances," she agreed cheerfully. "You've been in love with that kid since the day he walked his fine ass and threadbare jeans into your office and told you that as a 'full-time childcare specialist,' he believed in letting children choose their own interests rather than having their parents push them into things. Like he had any childcare experience to speak of back then." She chuckled. "Little did he know, he was talking to the boy who'd been made to do after-school academic enrichment like it was a full-time job." She patted my chest. "You were putty in his hands after that, Grant. Not that Brody's realized it."

I shook my head. Gwen was incorrigible, but she wasn't wrong. And yet...

"Those aren't the circumstances I was referring to, and you know it," I whispered testily. I darted a glance at Brody. He'd finished setting up snacks and looked like he was headed in this direction but was continually waylaid by parents wanting to chat with him. "And could you quiet down, at least a little? Brody probably feels awkward enough without overhearing you commenting on his 'fine ass.'"

Gwen surveyed my face and nodded once. "I was going to ask you how married life was going, but I guess that grumpy face is my answer, huh?"

"What?" I scowled. "No. It's going great. It's terrific. The school is happy. The girls seem happy. Brody seems happy."

"And you?"

"I'm happy, too." I snorted. "Obviously. Why wouldn't I be?" Other than intense, unrelenting sexual frustration, of course.

Humerus, radius, ulna...

She regarded me with one dark eyebrow raised, but I ignored her.

I glanced back down the field in time to see Brody peer over at me. Our eyes met, and Brody's eyelids fluttered a little in surprise. He sent me a goofy, awkward grin and a little wave that made my pulse race.

Carpal, metacarpal, phalanges.

The body had only two hundred and six bones, and if Brody kept being so damn unintentionally sexy, I was going to run out of them quickly.

I turned to Gwen and whispered low and fast, "Fine. If you must know, it's fucking *torture*, okay? It was bad enough before the whole marriage thing, but it's *so* much worse now. At least before, I knew I couldn't touch him or stare at him for too long. There were *rules*. Everyone knew he was my employee. But now..." I blew out a breath. "I've got this ring on my finger, and I like it. The girls expect us to sit next to each other on the sofa when we watch movie night. They expect me to give Brody a hug and a cheek kiss when I get home from work, just like I do with them. People think it's weird when I don't stand close enough to him, like at Back to School night. He *waves at me*." I ran a hand through my hair. "It's the best-worst thing that's ever happened to me, and I don't know what to do about it."

My dick was hard *constantly*. My skin tingled in anticipation of the slightest touch. My stomach had tied itself into a knot of sexual frustration. I wanted him so badly... and I still couldn't have him.

"Oh, sweetheart." Gwen shook her head. "Why don't you just tell him how you feel and put both of you out of your misery?"

I blinked at her, horrified. "Gwen, he's my *employee*. And Brody is a saint for agreeing to marry me in the first place. I'm not gonna make the situation even weirder by making unwanted sexual advances! Can you imagine?"

Her eyes widened. "Unwanted..." She shook her head firmly. "No. No, Grant, even *you* cannot be that oblivious. I refuse to believe it."

"*Excuse me*?"

"Oh, shit," she whispered, covering her mouth with one hand. "Or maybe you *can*. You really don't know, do you? Oh, honey."

"Gwen." I looked around us again. "Can you stop? People are looking in our direction, and Brody's going to come over here—"

"Yes," she interrupted quickly. "Yes, Brody *was* your employee, and I understood you not wanting to abuse your position. That probably makes you a really honorable person, with integrity or whatever." Gwen waved a hand, brushing aside honor and integrity like annoying flies. "But that's over now. You're not his boss; you're his husband. There's no power imbalance because he can leave whenever he wants and claim spousal support for a few years. It's in the prenup you signed, correct?"

"I... I suppose, yes," I agreed. I'd wanted to make sure he'd never regret the time he'd given up for my family, and I needed to know he'd be taken care of financially.

"Good. Then let me rock your world right now by informing you that Brody has wanted you *at least* as long as you've wanted him."

I shook my head and sipped my iced coffee. "That's ridiculous. I'm a decade older than he is. He likes some blue-eyed gym rat."

"Brody Kelly worships the ground you walk on. He looks at you like he wants to have your babies."

I choked on the coffee, nearly splattering it all over the Mountbatten golf shirt Mia had picked out for me that morning. "What?"

"He's always been mature, Grant. And what he went through with his parents matured him even faster. That's why you were so impressed with him in the first place. Remember?"

"But..." Brody had saved our household from chaos, and he'd been everything stable the girls had needed. I wasn't quite sure what I'd do without him. Just thinking about him wanting me back made my skin buzz and my heart beat erratically.

"Next time he talks to you," she hissed as Brody headed in our direction, "stop worrying about the way *you're* looking at *him* and notice the way he checks you out." She turned and opened her arms to wrap Brody in an enormous hug. "Brody, we were just talking about you! I was telling Grant that you're an absolute dream, and I don't know how Mountbatten ever ran this place without you."

"Oh." Brody blushed and glanced up at *me* before looking at Gwen. "Thank you. That's so sweet, but I'm really not doing much. Just helping out."

For a second, I wondered if Gwen could possibly be right, but...

God, what if she wasn't? What if I made him feel pressured? What if I said or did something that ruined everything? I wished that I had the ability to read emotions that seemed to come so easily to people like Gwen and Brody.

Then again, if Brody was that good at reading emotions, how come he couldn't see how I felt?

"They're getting ready to start," I said, pointing to Mia, who was standing in a gaggle of kids on one end of the field.

"Go, Mia!" Gwen shouted, and Mia waved back proudly.

Brody pulled out his cell phone to take a video of the game. "First soccer game at Mountbatten," he narrated excitedly. "And our Mia is decked out in her uniform, ready to do her part. Oh my gosh, Grant, look at them. How adorable are they in their little shin guards and cleats?"

My heart swelled at his happiness and the implication Mia was his, too. His love for the girls was like a living, breathing thing, and it lit up his face so much right then I wanted to take my own video. Of him.

The referee held a whistle in her mouth and tried to get a few players from each team to come to the center for the kickoff, and as I watched, I felt the smooth, hesitant slide of Brody's hand in mine. "Sorry. This okay?" he whispered. "Cleo's teacher is standing just behind us."

"Oh. Yeah, I guess." I purposefully did not look at Gwen's face because I didn't want to see her smug expression.

But as I watched Mia out on the field, the memory came to me of earlier this week, when Mia had been bragging at dinner about being "chosen" for the soccer team, though in reality, all of the kids who signed up got to play. No amount of Jacey explaining it convinced Mia she was less than supremely talented, and later that night, Jacey had begged Brody to intervene and explain things.

"Oh, no. No way," Brody had laughingly refused. "Everyone deserves to know they're an important part of a team, Jacey."

For the first time, I wondered... Did Brody ever question how important *he* was?

I squeezed his hand, and he glanced up at me questioningly. "I... I know I don't remember to say it often, Brody, but... Thank you for all that you do for our family. I don't know what the girls would do without you. I don't know what *I* would do without you. You really are amazing."

"Oh. Wow." Brody blinked, clearly stunned, and I felt foolish. Had I really never mentioned it before? Was it *that* much of a surprise?

My heart sank. Gwen was wrong. There was absolutely no way that Brody was interested in me, unless he somehow enjoyed men with the emotional aptitude of a root vegetable. This was all pretense.

Gwen's voice rang out, "Let's go, Chargers!" and Brody turned back toward Mia, phone camera at the ready. But he left his hand in mine, throughout the utter comical chaos of a six-year-old's soccer game, and when the Chargers scored and Brody gave me an impromptu hug, I wrapped my arms around him and soaked up every single moment.

If pretending Brody was mine was the closest I would get to the real thing, I was going to pretend as much as possible until it was gone.

~

My resolution on the soccer field seemed like a straightforward enough plan, but it only took a matter of hours for it to become complicated.

"Dad? How come you and Brody don't sleep in the same bed?"

"What?" I looked up from the bedtime story I was reading aloud and stared at Cleo, who was snuggled against my side on the sofa.

"Ella's dads sleep in the same bed," Mia said from my other side.

"And you used to sleep in the same bed with Mom when you were married," Cleo went on. "So why not you and Brody?"

"Uh. Well…" I began.

A sound like a restrained gasp alerted me to Brody's presence in the doorway of the living room. His eyes met mine, and his cheeks turned beet red.

"*Dad*?" Mia prompted.

"Yeah, Dad." Jacey gave me a shit-eating grin from the opposite sofa before turning the same smile on Brody. "Why don't you?"

Brody raised one eyebrow at Jacey, and she chuckled softly.

"The thing is, girls…" I scrambled to come up with a reasonable explanation, but the sight of a blushing Brody had fried my brain. *Sorry*, I mouthed with a helpless shrug.

"We do!" Brody lied, wading in to rescue me wearing a big, fake smile. "You just don't notice because we go to bed later than you and wake up earlier than you!"

"But how come your stuff isn't in Dad's closet?" Mia asked.

"Er. Lots of people have separate closets," I informed them.

"Okay, but when I went in there this morning, your phone charger and ChapStick were still on the nightstand," Cleo asked with a little frown.

"Yup. Yes." Brody nodded. "That's… that's a good point. With an easy explanation…" He gave me a hopeful look.

"Because we haven't had time to move things," I interjected smoothly. "Simple as that. Brody's so busy with his classes and your school, and I've been so busy at work, that we haven't had time to go through the whole process of moving his, uh… ChapStick," I finished uncertainly.

Jacey giggled behind her hand, and even Brody's eyes were alight with laughter.

"Oh." Mia sounded relieved. "So you'll do it this weekend, then?"

Brody's smile died, and he looked at me wide-eyed, but I didn't have a single good excuse why we couldn't…

My brain was far too full of all the reasons I really wished we *could.*

"Yes. We will," I agreed hoarsely. My lips tingled just from saying the words. "From now on, Brody and I will share a bedroom like other married couples. No problem at all."

Now it was Brody's turn to mouth *Sorry* at me, which was almost comical. There was no world in which Brody Kelly needed to be sorry for coming to my bed.

"Oh, phew," Cleo said with a relieved smile. "I thought maybe you were mad at Brody like the time you were mad at me for breaking Mia's night-light and said I couldn't sleep over in her room anymore."

I met Brody's eyes across the room. "No, sweetheart. I'm not mad at Brody. Quite the opposite, actually." I tugged at my shirt collar, but remembering Gwen's words earlier, I forced myself to meet his eyes and said decisively, "I'm *happy* to have Brody share my room."

Tension filled the room as the blush on Brody's cheeks streaked down his neck. His eyes held mine for a beat, then two, giving me a look I couldn't quite identify but which made my breath catch in my throat even so.

"S-same," he said in a rough voice, and though he addressed himself to my daughter, his eyes never moved from my face. "I like your dad, Cleo. A lot. That's why I married him. I'm *very* happy to share his room."

Is he saying...? Does he mean...?

Had Gwen actually been correct about this? Did Brody want me the way I wanted him?

Christ, what was I prepared to do about it if he did?

I was terrible with relationships and emotions. That hadn't changed. No one but Liza had ever put up with me for long, and in the end, she, too, had become so frustrated with me not being considerate enough, supportive enough, or emotionally aware enough as a partner that she'd been ready to end our marriage even before I'd begun exploring my sexuality.

But if Brody wanted to kiss me, was I going to refuse him?

One look at his face made my stomach clench with excitement and nerves, and I knew in that moment that I absolutely wouldn't.

Mia hopped in place on her sofa cushion. "Yes, but do you *loooove* each other?"

"Mia!" Cleo groaned. "Gross!"

Mia giggled so hard she flopped onto her side and began chanting, "Brody and Daddy sitting in a tree, K-I-S-S-I-N-G!" until Cleo bopped her over the head with a couch cushion.

Now Brody's wasn't the only face bright red with embarrassment. Thankfully, the girls were too distracted to ask any more questions.

"Hush," I told them sternly. "Only one story left before it's time to calm down and get in bed."

They fell quiet eventually, and I kept reading, but I could feel Brody's eyes on me the entire time, and I tried very hard not to think about how, shortly after *their* bedtime, it would be time for *me* to get in *my* bed... and for the first time in years, I would not be going alone.

I could guarantee there would be nothing calm about that.

6

BRODY

He wants me. Oh god, he wants me.

Does he? Maybe I misread the situation.

My brain was going a mile a minute while I brushed my teeth for the third time. Maybe Grant didn't really expect me to sleep in his room. What if his plan was simply for us to pretend?

I hated feeling unsure. And the last person I wanted to embarrass myself in front of was Grant. But at the same time, I wanted him enough to take the chance. Enough to embarrass myself if that's what it took to *get* that chance.

When I was clean from my toes to my teeth and sporting my least disgusting pajama pants and sleep tee, I made my way down the hall to Grant's bedroom. Worst-case scenario, he had a giant king-sized bed. We'd simply... share it. Platonically.

God, I hoped for the best-case scenario.

I knocked lightly on the door before pushing it open. "Um, Grant?"

"Yeah, come in," he said, poking his head out from the open bathroom door. He was wearing nothing but a bath towel around his waist and was wiping the last vestiges of toothpaste from his mouth with a hand towel. "Close the door, and make yourself comfortable."

Sure. *Comfortable.* As if that was possible right now.

I'd seen Grant's body before at the pool. His muscular chest covered in enough dark hair to make my fingers itch, the tight abs hidden beneath the barest layer of soft padding, his wide, rounded shoulders and toned biceps... he was hot as fuck. I knew certain women at the neighborhood club gossiped about who would be the lucky lady to become the next Mrs. Brighton. Several of them even gushed about their eagerness to simply be his next one-night stand.

And here I was, preparing to share his bed.

Possibly platonically.

Please don't let it be platonically.

When Grant ducked back into the bathroom, I stood halfway between the door and the end of the bed, shifting from foot to foot awkwardly. The room was big—bigger even than my own large suite—and decorated in a sophisticated, cozy shade of deep gray-green that I'd bet money had been Grant's sister's suggestion. During the day, the large picture windows here and over the tub in the bathroom looked out onto the peaceful, tree-lined backyard. The air smelled of Grant's sandalwood cologne, masculine and understated.

The space was incredibly familiar. I'd been in here a million times before, putting away laundry or dropping a fresh order of shaving balm on his vanity, but standing there knowing Grant was half-naked and only feet away? Yeah, that was new. And, I didn't mind admitting, it was a total mindfuck, even before I let myself imagine crawling up onto that tall bed, laying myself out on that plush comforter, and letting the man of my dreams—

"Hey," Grant said, leaning on the bathroom door.

I jumped at least a foot and gave a high-pitched squeal that would no doubt play on a loop in my brain at 3:00 a.m. every night for the rest of my existence. I pressed a hand to my chest to calm my racing heart and told my dick to slow its roll.

"Sorry," he said more gently. "I just wondered why you're still standing there." He came into the room wearing nothing but a pair of pajama pants that rode low on his lean hips. While I missed the sight of his curved leg muscles, there was plenty of territory to feast my eyes on from the waist up.

Enough to make my mouth go dry.

Think, Brody. He asked you a question.

I licked my lips. "I didn't, uh... I didn't know what, um, side you wanted me to..." There wasn't enough moisture for my tongue to complete the sentence, so it ended on a strange little click sound in my throat.

So suave. So attractive.

Fuck.

Grant's face softened as he walked toward me. "Are you okay? I don't mean to..." He waved a hand up and down in front of himself, indicating his naked torso, *like I wasn't already profoundly aware of it.* "I prefer to sleep this way, and I figured maybe it'd be best if we were just... ourselves. But I can put a shirt on—" He broke off at my frantic head shake. "Or we could talk about things? I don't expect anything from you, Brody. I know I'm not the sort of guy you're attracted to. I would never—"

"Kiss me!" I managed to bark out. That wasn't at all what I'd have planned to say, if my mind were capable of planning, but I couldn't—didn't want to—take it back, either, so I went with it. "I mean, I think we should kiss. I mean. I mean, for... um... purposes of... making our relationship convincing? I mean, not that I don't want... I mean, you *are* the sort of guy I find attractive. You, personally, I mean. Not other guys like you. And we could... I mean, if you wanted..."

Great. The words "I mean" no longer have any meaning at all. Good job, Brody.

Click. Click. I tried to swallow, but it was impossible. And apparently, someone had stolen all the oxygen in the room because breathing had become tricky, too.

Grant's gaze grew more intent, like I was a puzzle he was trying to solve.

Good luck, I wanted to tell him. *If you figure it out, I would love some insight.*

I wanted Grant Brighton—wanted to sleep with him—enough

that I'd give up just about anything. But the ease and camaraderie we shared? The comfortable closeness that had made me feel like I *fit* somewhere for the first time since my family had been taken from me? No, I wasn't sure I could give that up and have it replaced with this halting awkwardness, not even for the most phenomenal, life-changing sex.

Grant stepped closer until he was definitely in my personal space. My fingers wanted to tangle in his chest hair so badly that the force of restraining myself was nearly painful.

"Oh, god, you're the sexiest person I've ever met," I blurted, then immediately regretted it. "Sorry," I whisper-croaked. "I'm probably the most awkward person *you've* ever met."

Grant put his hands on my upper arms and squeezed gently before running them up over my shoulders to cup my neck and then my face. "You're the most *beautiful* person I've ever met," he corrected in a low voice.

For a moment, I wondered if someone had replaced reality with a Brody's All-Time Greatest Fantasies reel. *Had he really just said that? The words made me dizzy and desperate.*

"Please," I whispered, unwilling to risk any misunderstanding. With him here, this close, and his hands on me, I didn't want to waste my chance. "Please."

His lips landed on mine featherlight, a soft brush for a split second of yearning before our mouths suddenly remembered how hungry they were and the kiss turned desperate and feral.

"Oh fuck," Grant spoke against my lips. "I knew it would be like this. *Fuck.*"

I whimpered and pressed my body against his, wrapping my arms around his back and splaying my hands wide to hold him close.

We kissed like our very lives depended on getting as deep into each other's mouths as possible. His big hands gripped my head, and the warm breath exhaled through his nose lit up my skin everywhere it landed. His sexy scent—sandalwood and *Grant*—bonded itself to my DNA, and I knew that for the rest of my life, nothing else would ever get me as instantly, undeniably aroused.

Grant's hands moved down to wrap around me. One strayed to the back of my neck to hold me in place while the other moved down to cup my ass and squeeze. I could feel my dick leaking, dampening the front of my pajamas, but I didn't care. I couldn't stop making noises of desperation, of desire, of submission.

Whatever Grant Brighton wanted to do to me was going to be my new favorite regardless of what it was.

"Want you so fucking much," he growled before moving down to nip the edge of my jaw before sucking the tender skin of my neck between his teeth.

"Yes," I breathed. "Anything. Please."

"I've wanted you for so long, Brody. Christ. Be sure. Please be sure you want this with me. I don't—"

"I am," I said quickly. "Fuck, *of course* I am. It's *you*. You can have whatever you want, Grant. Anything. Always. *Please.*"

I knew I was repeating myself, but I'd lost the ability to be articulate the moment he'd stepped into the room.

I was a vessel of pure *want* now, and for the first time ever, I didn't want to hide any part of that wanting.

I knew Grant would worry about our age difference and the fact that I'd been his employee—if not now, then later. I needed him to know that I wasn't just going along with this. I fucking *ached* for it.

I didn't want him to stop.

And I didn't ever want him to regret.

"What do you want?" he said, moving both hands down to grasp my ass with those strong, life-saving hands. "I want you to feel good. What would make you feel good?"

Shit. Now that the *regret* word had entered my head, I couldn't stop thinking about it. I needed to move things along, to let the wanting take me over again.

"Naked," I said through heaving breaths. "You, me, no clothes."

The low rumble of his laugh vibrated through my chest before he pulled away to lift my T-shirt over my head.

"Yes," he said simply before lowering his mouth to trail kisses down to one of my nipples. "God, yes." After a strong suck I felt all the way down to my balls, he lifted me up like I weighed nothing and sat me down on the edge of his giant bed.

I stared up at him, gloriously sexy and flushed, eyes wide and pupils blown, watching me with one hundred percent of his incredible focus, and I knew this was the moment I'd dreamed of.

I could run my hand over his thick hair the way I'd imagined.

Take his mouth with mine until he was moaning.

Strip off his pajama pants and worship his hardness with my lips and tongue and hands.

Live my fantasy.

I sucked in a deep breath... and froze.

"Brody?" Grant sensed my hesitation immediately. He clasped my cheek with one broad palm. "Talk to me."

"I want you so much. I'm scared of messing everything up," I blurted.

7

GRANT

I hadn't thought it was possible to crave Brody Kelly more than I already did, but hearing those words from his mouth proved me wrong.

He was nervous—highly ironic since that should have been *my* role here, as the older and probably less experienced of the two of us—but no matter how much I questioned emotions in other areas of my life, there wasn't a doubt in my mind that Brody wanted this as badly as I did. This mattered to him... maybe even as much as it mattered to me.

For the first time, I didn't have to think about the bones of the body when I was with him. I could let myself look my fill and want him without restraint.

"You're not going to mess anything up." I brushed his hair back from his forehead and leaned in to kiss the edge of his mouth. "You couldn't. I want you so badly I can barely think straight. But I need you to talk to me. Tell me what you want and what you don't. I don't want to do anything that makes you uncomfortable."

His cheeks were bright red, and the tips of his ears matched. His lips were slick from kissing, and his nose was pink from my beard scruff. He was devastatingly sexy like this, half-naked and in my bed.

"I want everything with you," he blurted. "But I don't know how to... to *be*."

A large part of me wanted to fixate on the word *everything*—was he saying that nothing was off the table for him tonight sexually? Or did he mean that he wanted a full-blown relationship?—but I wouldn't let myself get distracted. My priority was making Brody feel comfortable in this moment.

I stepped between his knees and loosely wrapped my arms around him. "Explain."

He swallowed hard. "I want you to take control, but I don't know how much experience you have with other guys, so maybe I should take control? But then you seem like you're doing pretty good so far." He laughed nervously. "So I guess I'm just caught up in a second-guessing cycle. Which makes me feel stupid. And then I worry you'll think I'm too young and silly for you." He let out a shuddering breath. "I worry you'll... regret this."

Brody's eyes angled down to my chest, and I hated that. I cradled his jaw in both hands and tilted his face up.

"I don't worry that you're too young for me. But I do worry that I'm too old for you," I admitted. "You're not silly, and you're sure as hell not stupid. Christ, you're the most capable, dependable person I know."

His eyes widened. "You... you work with a team of doctors."

I cracked a smile. "And my opinion stands."

Brody huffed out a laugh and lifted his hands to caress my wrists, holding my hands against his cheeks. The simple action made me feel so absurdly good I couldn't help but lean in and take another quick taste of his mouth.

"As for my experience with guys, I have more than enough to understand the basics." Even though sex with Brody felt like it was going to be outside the realm of my experience entirely. "I can take control. I do it every day at work, and I like it. I want to take care of you tonight," I admitted. "If you're good with that."

Brody's eyes kindled with heat. "Yeah. Yeah, I'm *great* with that."

I nodded once. "And the only way I'm going to regret tonight,

Brody, is if you don't enjoy yourself *entirely*. I'm not always the most observant, so you need to tell me what you're thinking. Fair?"

He nodded slowly. His gaze dropped to my mouth, and his eyes narrowed with something like challenge as he licked his lips. "Yeah. Okay. Fair."

"So, tell me..." I dropped my voice an octave to a low purr and pressed in closer, eliminating the space between us. "What are you thinking right now?"

His eyes met mine, a little bashful but still defiant. "I'm, ah... I'm thinking of your experience with *other guys*."

Friendly, sweet Brody practically spat the last words, and a bubble of startled laughter rose in my throat. He was *jealous*? Christ, I liked that. Possibly too much.

I pulled Brody against me and stripped the blankets down the bed in one desperate movement. Then I pushed him down until his back hit the mattress and reached for the waistband of his pajama pants to pull them off. "How about instead of thinking about me with other people, you just lie back and enjoy me with *you*?"

His dick was already rock hard, but it jumped when I drew the fabric down over it. He groaned and squeezed his eyes closed before muttering, "*Don't come yet. Don't ruin it. Jesus, hold it together.*"

It took me a second to realize that he was talking to himself and not to me, and I found myself close to laughter once more.

Had I ever laughed during sex? If so, I couldn't remember it. But then, with Brody laid out before me like a feast, I couldn't manage to think of anyone else at all.

I wanted to fuck him. There was no doubt about that. But I was quickly realizing I wanted a whole hell of a lot more than that with Brody, too. He was sexy as hell but also endearing and adorable. One taste wasn't going to be enough.

He's yours now. You can taste him more than once, some feral, caveman part of me—a lobe of my brain I'd never heard from before—pointed out. And the thought should have been ludicrous, given our agreement, given my own relationship limitations, but it was damn tempting to listen. To claim this gorgeous man in truth.

I put my hands under his knees and yanked him closer to the edge of the bed. He gave a startled cry as his dick bounced, and my mouth watered.

"Oh, no, you're not going to come yet," I agreed silkily. "You're going to do exactly what I tell you. And you won't come until I say."

Brody's gasp went directly to my dick, and I didn't hesitate. I leaned down and ran the flat of my tongue up his silky shaft. The noise he let out from his throat made me even harder than I already was. I quickly shucked off my own pajama pants and finished pulling his off until we were both blessedly naked.

Brody's thigh muscles contracted under my hands while I continued to lick and kiss his cock for long moments until he was dripping wet and canting his hips upward, begging for relief. But instead of taking him in my mouth the way we both clearly wanted, I nudged his legs further apart until they were splayed wide across my sheets and dropped my mouth lower so I could lick and fondle his balls.

"*Oh, fuckkkkkk,*" he moaned. One arm flopped over his face, hiding his eyes, while the other grabbed the sheet over his head, twisting it so hard one of the corners popped off the mattress.

The salty-sweet taste of him was addicting. I wanted more. More of his taste, his touch, his scent, his presence.

"Please," he begged. "*Grant.*"

I was sure I'd heard my first name on his lips at some point before but certainly never like this, tinged with need and desperation. It was funny how that single word could break through the last barriers in my mind and make me feel so damn desirable.

"What are you thinking now, Brody?" I demanded. "Tell me."

"I... oh, god. I'm thinking..."

I licked him from root to tip, and he bucked again as I lapped up the precum pooled at his slit.

"Tell me," I commanded, my words blowing hot over his damp skin. "Don't be shy."

"I want you so much," he blurted. "I've wanted you for so long. I really want you to take your time, but I also really want you to suck me. But I also don't want you to suck me because if you do, I'll come, and if I come, this will be over. But mostly I want you to suck me. Just... *suck me*," he wailed.

My brain caught and spun on the idea that he'd wanted me for a long time, that we could have been together like this months or even years ago. I'd thought I'd known everything about the man beneath me, but now I was glimpsing hidden facets of my competent, cheerful, occasionally awkward Brody. And I liked them every bit as much.

He ran his fingers through my hair and tugged, forcing my head up so his eyes met mine. "Please, Grant," he begged again.

Okay, maybe I liked these new facets best of all.

I held his eyes as I lowered my head to his cock and greedily sucked him in.

If Brody had been a live wire before, he was a star gone supernova once my mouth was on him. He babbled and chanted, imploring me not to *ever stop*, insisting that I *do it again, just like that*, crooning my name over and over like it was the filthiest curse he knew and a plea to a higher power. His legs flailed off the bed, and his hands came to rest on my head, not to pull or push, but like he needed an anchor in a storm.

Like he trusted me to be that for him.

"I... I'm so close," he whispered insistently.

I lurched up his body to kiss him on the mouth, tumbling us both back onto the bed in a way that brushed our bare cocks together, and I hissed at the contact. We worked our way fully onto the bed, scrambling across the sheets without breaking our kiss. It was mutual desperation: hands and mouths seeking as much of each other as we could get, as if the slow-burn wick of our wanting had suddenly been doused with fuel.

I'd never felt so undone. I'd never felt so free.

My brain scrambled to decide what I wanted more: quick frot, mutual blow jobs, or the sweet, tight feel of Brody's ass around me as I sank inside of him. Either way, I wasn't going to last. Just thinking of all the things I wanted to do to him—*with* him—was enough to make my balls tighten.

"What do you want, sweetheart?" I asked against the side of his face. Sweat plastered his hair to his skin, and his eyes were glassy. "Tell me now."

"You. Want to come. Want to come with you."

"Do it," I said, my voice wrecked from sex and need. "I want to see you."

I took us both in hand, pinning him to the bed with my legs and chest while I did my best to stroke us off. My mouth crushed his while I took everything I wanted from his kiss. His breaths came fast and shallow, little gasps with muttered curses thrown in.

His dick felt amazing against mine. I moved my hand down to gently squeeze his balls while continuing to thrust against him. Our cocks were spit-slick and hot, so it took me a minute to realize he was coming.

"Grant! Oh god. Fuck. *Fuck.*" His head tilted back into the pillow, and a tendon stuck out on his exposed neck. I latched onto it and sucked, taking his release and using it to bring myself off all over his belly.

I lay there trying not to crush him as the aftershocks of my orgasm washed over me. My mouth lay open against his sweaty neck, and I teased his skin lightly with my tongue.

Brody's hands moved up and down my back and into my hair. His legs wrapped around me to hold me close.

"Want to do that again. Soon," he said in a lazy voice that indicated he was already close to sleep. He chuckled. "Soon."

"Your wish is my command." Every muscle in my body sang from exertion, and logically, I knew we wouldn't be able to do anything like that again for hours at least, but he felt so good against me that my cock was already trying to rally.

I'd thought I had a pretty solid understanding of what married sex was supposed to be like. But it turned out, when you were having sex with the right person—the one you craved above all others—it wasn't boring or mechanical in the slightest. In fact, it was magic.

I placed one more kiss on his lips before pulling away.

"Don't go," he said, eyes opening wide with worry like I was going to get up and leave forever.

"I won't," I promised. Just like before, I wasn't sure exactly how long he was asking for... but I decided it didn't matter. I would stay with Brody for as long as I possibly could. "I just want to start a shower for us. Then I'm going to change the sheets and put you back in this bed with me." I brushed the damp hair from his forehead.

His worry changed to relief and then to a brilliant grin. "Because you want to take care of me tonight?"

"Because you're my husband," I said, tasting the strange words on my tongue. "Your place is here in our bed. If you want it to be."

His smile was shy. "I definitely want it to be."

I turned to head toward the bathroom just as he whispered the word *Husband*.

I wondered if it tasted as sweet and precious on his lips as it had on mine.

8

BRODY

Hot water streamed down my body, but all I could feel was the warm, firm press of Grant's hand on my stomach and the solid length of his tall frame against my back.

I was naked in the shower, after the most incredible sexual experience of my entire life, with Dr. Brighton, my boss and crush... *and husband.* I'd be convinced it was a dream if not for the very solid platinum band on my finger... and the matching one on Grant's.

He'd surprised me with matching rings the day after we'd learned everyone in the neighborhood had discovered our "secret" marriage. "Might as well go all in," he'd joked as he'd slid the shiny metal onto my left hand. He'd looked nervous as he did it—like he expected that to be the final straw that made me say, "Heck no! This charade is over." Little did he know, he was just handing me another brick that I was using to build a fairy-tale castle... even though I knew I wouldn't be able to live in it for long.

Grant pressed a kiss to my temple. "You're asleep on your feet. Long day."

More like a long, incredible evening. But I wasn't going to say that.

Instead, I murmured agreement, then asked, "Do you have to go to work tomorrow?" I hoped I didn't sound as needy as I felt. All I wanted to do was spend a lazy Sunday at home with him and the girls, pretending we were one big happy family.

"Nah. A doctor at Mass General wanted to set up a video call for a consult, but I told them it would have to be Monday. I promised the girls I'd make a big breakfast and help Cleo bake the cookies for her Robotics Club meet-up tomorrow afternoon." He sounded far prouder that his daughter had asked for his help than that a colleague at a hospital across the country wanted his advice, which squeezed my heart. Even a couple of years ago, he would have stuck to the thing he knew he was good at, which did not involve anything in the kitchen... or with his daughters. "What about you? Are you going to be able to join us, or do you have work to do?"

I had work—a ton of work, actually, between school assignments and the long process of getting my fledgling company up and running—but wild horses couldn't keep me away from a perfect family day like he described. "Nah, I'm good. I can do my schoolwork after the girls are in bed tomorrow night."

He frowned as he shut off the water and reached for a thick towel to dry me off with. "Didn't you say you had a project to finish in Probability and Statistics?"

For some reason, hearing Grant refer to my very boring class made me hot for him again. He was so fucking *thoughtful.* "Mmhm, but it's fine. It'll be quick since I already know what I want the project to be. Don't worry about it."

He finished rubbing me down with the towel and started on himself. "If you need quiet time tomorrow to work on it—"

"I don't," I said quickly. "I promise. Besides, I've been looking forward to seeing what Cleo's idea of robot-shaped cookies is."

He followed me into the bedroom and hooked a finger in the waistband of my pajama pants, which dangled from the bedside lamp, where one of us had thrown them. He held them out to me with a wry smile that made me blush, but when I tried to grab them, he used them to haul me against him. "As much as I wish I could hold you naked against me like this all night..."

"...we might have visitors," I finished, my voice hoarse.

He grinned, and we shared a look of perfect understanding.

It was moments like this, where the connection between us was so clear and palpable, that it was hard to remind myself it wasn't real. Now that we'd been together, now that I'd let him take control of my body and bring me indescribable pleasure, it was nearly impossible.

After pulling on his own pajamas, Grant turned toward the bed... and flushed adorably. "This is a mess."

He was right. The fitted sheet had popped off one corner of the mattress, and the flat sheet was a sweat-damp ball thrown off to one side.

"I don't think I've ever..." He swallowed and blinked at me.

"Never trashed a bed during sex?" I teased, unable to stomach the feelings his sweet insecurity raised in me. "That can't be right, Dr. Brighton."

His blush deepened as he began to efficiently strip the bed. I grabbed a new set of sheets from the linen closet in the bathroom, and the two of us worked together wordlessly to finish the task.

At length, he said quietly, "It's... different with men."

I nodded slowly as I slipped a pillow into a fresh case. I didn't want to startle him in case he was in the mood to open up to me. "Different bad or different good?"

He shrugged. "It's not really a good or bad thing, but I..." Grant's eyes flicked over to me before looking away again. "I liked it. With you. I... I like being able to..."

My heart felt like a blender on too high a setting. If I wasn't careful, it was going to turn everything to a mushy pulp. "Being able to...?" I asked gently.

"Let go. Be a little rough. Not worry about..." His eyes flicked up again, but this time, they stayed on mine. "About what you'd think of me if I..." He let out a soft chuckle. "If I lose control."

My chest pinched. I wanted to tell him he could let go with me anytime, but more than that, I wanted to tell him he should never be afraid of letting go in bed. If he was with a partner who didn't like it, well then, he was with the wrong partner.

"I like it, too," I said instead. "*A lot.*"

He smiled and reached for the fresh fitted sheet before unfurling it in the air between us. We continued to make the bed together, a strangely intimate moment of domesticity I liked a little too much.

Once the bed was made, we fell into it and naturally gravitated toward each other until I was pressed tightly against Grant with his fingers drawing light shapes along my back.

"Thank you for being here," Grant said in a low voice. "In... in every way."

I leaned up and pressed a kiss to the edge of his jaw. It wasn't enough, so I moved my mouth and pressed another one to his chin, and then his cheek... and nose, and eyebrows, grateful that I got to live this moment. That I was able to kiss him as much as I liked. Before long, we were kissing each other with a hunger I'd never felt before. It made me nervous and excited all at once. Why did this feel so different with him than with anyone I'd ever been with?

Grant arched up into me, pressing his hard cock against my stomach. I wanted him again, only this time, I wanted more.

"Can I suck you off this time?" I breathed against his throat. "Please?"

I wanted to feel the heavy weight of him on my tongue, get to know the hot length of him, the taste of him.

The deep rumble of his laugh vibrated through my chest. "Has any man ever said no to that question?"

I moved down his chest, licking and sucking everywhere, learning the planes of his body and memorizing it all in case this was suddenly yanked away from me. It was still unclear to me what his intentions were long-term. Did he think this was only for the rest of the school year? Or longer? What would it take for him to consider something more? Something permanent?

When I got to the waistband of his pajama pants, I slowed down to tease him. I wanted him desperate and begging, writhing with need the way I felt every time he touched me.

"What..." He sucked in a breath as my tongue ran a lazy path down his happy trail. "What are you doing?"

I smiled against his skin but didn't answer. Grant's fingers threaded into my hair. "Fucking Christ, that... that's amazing." The groan he let out went straight to my dick, and my mouth filled with saliva.

I wasn't sure which of us I'd been teasing most.

I pulled down the waistband and inhaled before sucking the tip of his cock into my mouth and swirling my tongue around it. When he'd started sucking me off earlier, I'd lost my mind. I wanted to give him that same feeling. I wanted him to lose himself.

In me.

The noises he made as I licked and sucked and stroked him sent me right to the edge of my own release as well. My mind was a vat of colorful static as I raced toward both of our completions.

"Brody, baby, *fuck*," he cried, thrusting into my mouth and tightening his fingers in my hair. As soon as the warm tang of his orgasm hit the back of my throat, I shoved my hand into my own pants and stroked myself once, twice, and then I was coming.

The colorful static burst into shooting stars as the muscles in my body contracted deliciously and then relaxed. The sound of my ragged breathing filled the room as I rolled off him onto my back on the bed.

When Grant reached over to twist his fingers in mine, I felt the hard, cool metal of his wedding ring. My stomach flipped a little, and my cock gave a final twitch.

Grant Brighton was mine, for better or for worse.

"Another shower?" he asked with an eyebrow wiggle that made my breath hitch. "Then sleep. Before long, it'll be morning, and one of three demanding young women will be waking us up."

I grinned. So far, marriage to Grant was all for the *better*, I decided as I let him lead me back to the shower. Entirely, wonderfully better.

But when morning came, the demanding woman who woke us was not one of our girls... and things took a decided turn for the *worse*.

9

———

GRANT

"What the hell is going on here?"

The angry voice startled me out of a deep slumber, and I cracked my eyes open, squinting against the sunlight streaming through the window.

My first thought was that waking with Brody Kelly's warm body entwined with mine, his tousled hair fanned out on my pillow, and his adorably sleepy green eyes blinking up at me was one of the highlights of my life, and I wanted to remember that moment forever.

In the next second, my brain processed the familiar voice, and I looked past Brody to the irate woman who'd invaded our bedroom and was currently glaring at us from the doorway.

"Liza?" I croaked. My brain scrambled to put pieces of two seemingly disparate puzzles together.

They didn't fit.

"You can't be serious," she said, moving closer to the bed and peering at Brody like he was a specimen. "The *babysitter*, Grant?"

I instinctively yanked the duvet up to Brody's shoulders to shield him from her. He tried to pull away, but I tightened my arm around him to hold him exactly where he was—with me.

"Liza, I don't know what you're doing here, but get out of my bedroom. Now."

"You've lost your mind." She addressed her words to me, but her eyes didn't stray from Brody, and as he stared up at her, I felt him begin to shake.

"I'm sorry, I..." he began in a small voice that twisted my gut. Brody had *nothing* to apologize for. Not one damn thing.

I pushed up on one elbow so I was leaning over him, suddenly entirely awake—and angry as hell. "You're not listening. Get the *fuck* out of my room, Liza," I reiterated in a low voice so the girls wouldn't hear through the open door. "Right the fuck now."

She peered over me at Brody. "What the heck were you thinking. He looks about twelve years old—"

I leaped over Brody and lunged out of the bed in only my pajama pants, crowding Liza back toward the door and out to the hallway. As soon as she crossed the threshold, I closed the door behind her and locked it.

"We are *not* done talking about this, Grant!" she yelled through the door. "I'll be waiting for you downstairs."

My forehead hit the cool wood of the door as I exhaled.

Fuck.

What the hell was Liza doing here? I had expected her to hear about my marriage from one of the girls—that was how I'd heard about her wedding to Elias a few years back, after all—but I hadn't anticipated that it would lead to an impromptu visit, let alone to her demanding explanations for things that were none of her damn business. She knew the girls adored Brody, she knew I trusted him, and she'd never had an issue with him being in their lives before, so her outrage wasn't about Brody himself; it had to be about me.

Well, if she'd come to berate me for marrying someone a decade younger than me, she could fuck right off because I didn't want to hear it. Not after last night. Besides fatherhood, this fake marriage to Brody was the best, most *real* thing in my life, and I'd cling to it as long as he'd let me.

"You okay?" Brody's voice was soft and unsure. I turned to see him standing awkwardly in the middle of the room.

I moved to him quickly and cupped his face. "I'm fine. But I'm so sorry about that. *Christ.* I had no idea she was coming. I'll ask her to leave," I said impulsively.

Brody's raised eyebrow said he knew as well as I did that I was lying. I'd never tell my daughters their mother wasn't allowed in their own home.

But still. There needed to be rules.

"Better yet, I'll talk to the girls," I corrected. "Explain that they can't just let her in here without advanced notice. This is our home. We deserve privacy."

"Yeah. Okay." Brody nodded slowly, but his gaze was fixed on the closed door behind me. "She's really beautiful, huh? Liza, I mean."

"Yes," I agreed distractedly. Objectively speaking, Liza was tanned and blonde and attractive, and I'd heard Gwen say on many occasions that she envied Liza's trim figure. At that moment, though, my ex-wife was a huge complication who'd barged into my private space and disturbed an intimate moment between me and my husband, so I was not disposed to think kind thoughts like Brody was. He was a far better person than I.

I knew I needed to get dressed and compose myself so I could go downstairs to deal with her, so I reluctantly let Brody go and headed for the walk-in closet to grab a pair of jeans and my favorite button-down.

"I've seen pictures of her, of course," Brody said, still staring blankly at the door. "Jacey once showed me your wedding album and asked if she and Liza looked alike. And I've seen pictures of her from the times she's come to visit or when the girls have gone to see her. But photos don't do her justice. There's just this... *air* about her. Confident and bold. She must have so many amazing stories about her life."

"Yup. Millions." I'd heard many from the girls over the years, though at the moment, I couldn't remember a single one. I pulled on my jeans and tossed my pajama pants on the bed, determinedly ignoring how much I wanted to crawl back into it—with Brody—and keep the world at bay a little longer.

Brody sucked in a breath and shook himself like he was waking from a trance. "Right. Okay. I'll skip breakfast," he said matter-of-factly. He located his T-shirt from the foot of the bed, where I'd thrown it the night before, and pulled it on. "You guys will need some space to... talk and whatnot."

"Oh." I glanced up from fastening my shirt buttons with a frown. My whole body revolted at the idea of Brody not being with me—preferably pressed right up alongside me—but logically speaking, he was probably right.

Liza was not normally inclined to emotional outbursts or name-calling, but she hadn't been acting like herself that morning. I needed to have a mature, rational discussion with her about boundaries, and if she made a single snarky comment to Brody or even threw a less-than-friendly glance in his direction, I'd end up raising my voice. I wouldn't be able to stop myself. And that would be unproductive.

I sighed. "You're right. That would probably be a good idea." I reached for his hands and clasped them tightly, staring down at him in wonder. "Thank you for being so thoughtful. I'll have Jacey bring you some coffee, and I'll come find you when it's time for cookie making later, okay?"

Brody pulled his hands away and turned to tidy the bed. "Nonsense. Cleo will want Liza to help with the cookies." He plumped the pillows and tossed a happy-go-lucky grin over his shoulder, though his eyes didn't quite meet mine. "The girls will have a *thousand* things to tell her. Every single detail about school, and their friends, and Mia's swimming trophy from camp, and Cleo's progress report, and the boy Jacey likes—"

"Jacey likes a boy?" I frowned. "Since when?"

Brody huffed out a laugh and moved briskly to the other side of the bed, forcing me to step aside. "All in all, it's probably better if I give you guys the day to yourselves. I'll head to Fen's. I have a *ton* of work to do."

"But—" I frowned harder. "I thought you said yesterday that your project wouldn't be much work at all. That you could get it done tonight. That you wanted to spend the day with us." I didn't want to be selfish, especially if it meant distracting him from important work, but I felt unexpectedly needy where Brody was concerned. I wanted him with me. Always.

"I did want to! I *do*. But..." Brody paused with my pillow in his hands. "It's not every day that their mom is in town," he said softly. "The girls miss her. They deserve to have as much family time as possible, without distraction."

Brody's voice sounded tight, an emotion I couldn't quite name... at least until I noticed that his fingers were gripping the pillow so hard his knuckles had turned white, and the reason for his strange behavior dawned on me.

Fuck, I was an idiot.

Brody had lost his own mother—his whole family, in fact—in a terrible car accident. Liza's arrival had probably triggered some latent grief. So of *course* he wanted the girls to spend as much time with their own mom as they could. He loved them and wanted the best for them. That was the sort of selfless person he was.

I sighed again and tried to get over my unreasonable disappointment. In truth, as annoyed as I was by Liza's appearance, the girls *would* be over the moon to see their mom. Despite tons of FaceTime calls and texts, in addition to her irregular visits, they didn't get nearly enough time with her.

"Thank you, Brody," I said again, hoping he knew how deeply I meant it. "For being so understanding after... everything. And if you want to talk about—" *Your parents, your feelings, your past.* "—things, we can do that. Okay?"

His lips tightened, and he gave me a strange smile. "Sure. I'll see you later." He walked toward the door.

I blinked, and my stomach tightened. Okay, so maybe he didn't want to talk about anything. For all my degrees and experience putting people back together physically, it was patently obvious to anyone who knew me that my skills did not extend to emotions.

Still, it felt odd that he hadn't kissed me goodbye, or given me one of his sweet Brody smiles, or in any way acknowledged what we'd shared the night before.

He's sad, Grant, I reminded myself. *This isn't about you.*

Still, I couldn't help but call his name as he reached for the doorknob, hoping my voice didn't sound quite as desperate and needy as I felt.

He turned. "Yes?"

I crossed the distance between us in three steps and pulled him against me, probably a little too roughly, taking his lips with mine in a way I hoped said, *"This isn't over,"* but more likely came across as, *"Mine, mine, mine."*

I kissed him hungrily and without apology, and when he pulled back, he looked dazed and wobbly. The caveman part of me—the part that Brody had awakened—growled in satisfaction.

"See you later," I said roughly before closing my mouth to keep the taste of him inside.

When I loped down the back stairs to the kitchen, the girls were crowded around the table, asking Liza a million and one questions, just as Brody had predicted. They were happy and bubbly, talking over one another, and Mia had even climbed on her lap to let Liza brush the nighttime tangles out of her hair, which was usually something only Brody was allowed to do.

"Good morning," I said, ruffling Cleo's hair.

Liza gave me a long look I couldn't interpret, but all she said was "I made coffee. Help yourself."

So we'd be postponing our reckoning until the girls were distracted? *Fine.*

I went directly to the pot and poured myself a cup. But just as I pulled the mug up to my lips to take the first sip, I noticed a giant pile of luggage and boxes crowding the hallway by the front door.

I set my mug back down on the countertop.

When Liza came to visit, she stayed at a hotel. The one time she hadn't, shortly after our divorce, things had been strained and awkward, and she'd never suggested it again.

Also, that was a monumental pile of stuff. Not a suitcase and a camera bag, like one might expect for a couple of weeks' stay, but at least seven suitcases and two large boxes, one of which was labeled "equipment" in large black letters, and the other "house stuff."

My heart rate accelerated. This was not "visit" luggage; it was "moving back" luggage.

I met Liza's eyes across the kitchen. "How long are you staying?" I asked carefully. Her answer might change... everything.

She looked away. "I'm not sure. I'm looking for a new project. I'd like to find something here in California."

"Really?" Jacey said excitedly. "Mom! That would be so cool!"

Brody had just entered the kitchen, his backpack slung over one shoulder. He froze for a beat before continuing to the coffee maker to fill his travel mug.

"Brody, this is the girls' mother, Liza. Liza, this is Brody Kelly." I swallowed before adding, "My husband." Those words seemed almost too precious to share, especially after Liza's attitude upstairs, but I was proud of my connection to Brody. I was proud that, for a while at least, I got to be his husband. Claiming him was a privilege.

Jacey turned her brilliant smile to Brody and me.

Liza inspected Brody from head to toe. She lifted her chin several inches. "I've heard a lot about you from the girls, Brody. But I hadn't heard about your... relationship." She glanced at me. "Quite the surprise."

Brody's cheeks turned a mottled kind of red, but he didn't smile... or rise to her bait. "Nice to meet you finally, Liza. The girls have talked about you for years also. They love you very much." He cleared his throat and hefted his backpack higher on his shoulder. "Well. Enjoy your day, everyone."

"Stay," I blurted, not wanting to part with him. "At least for pancakes."

Liza smiled widely. "Yes, do stay. There's plenty of room. And Grant makes the best pancakes."

The red streaked down Brody's neck, and his fingers tightened on his backpack strap. "I know he does. But, uh... I have work to do, so I'll leave you to catch up." His eyes flicked from Liza to me and then to the girls. "You all have fun."

"We will," Liza assured him. "Oh! Brody, before you go, could you help with my luggage? The cab driver helped me bring it into the front hall, but it's going to require someone *young* and strong to bring it upstairs. It'll be nothing for a kid like you." Her smile sharpened. "I'd appreciate it."

Brody's face turned beet red in an instant at the "kid" comment and then lost all color just as quickly. He glanced at me. "Upstairs? Where upstairs?"

I shook my head once. "You can't stay here, Liza. We don't have room. I can help you find a short-term rental, or I can ask Gwen if she has space—"

"But, Dad." Cleo frowned. "Can't Mom stay in Brody's old room?"

"No," I said, anger making the word come out more firmly than necessary. There was a tension in the air between Liza and Brody that I didn't understand. I wasn't quite sure what had caused it or how to interpret it, but it had blanketed Brody's sunshine, and that was unacceptable.

"Grant, I'd really prefer to stay with my *family*," Liza said, cuddling Mia closer, and I nearly bit my tongue against a sharp retort.

Brody gave Cleo a reassuring smile. "You're right, sweetie. That's a great idea. Your mom can have my room." He looked at me. "I can just stay at Fen's for a while."

"Perfect," Liza began.

"It is *not* perfect," I growled. I turned to pin Brody with a glare. "You're not staying at Fen's. You're staying *here* in your *home*. With me. In *our* room. Because we're *married*, remember? That's not up for debate."

Brody's eyes widened, but his cheeks turned the rosy, sunset-pink color that meant everything was okay on my personal horizon. "Okay, then. I'll... see you later."

In two steps, I grabbed him again and kissed him wildly, heedless of everything around us. "Please be careful," I murmured against his lips. "Text me later. Okay?"

He nodded and walked unsteadily out the door.

When I turned back to the table, the three girls were grinning—Mia had clapped her hand over her mouth to stifle a giggle—and even Liza watched me intently, a little frown between her eyes.

I wanted to talk to her, but there was no time. The girls hungrily demanded pancakes and bacon, and after I'd cleaned up, Liza and Cleo were already pulling out supplies for robot cookies. By the time the oddly shaped robot cookies were cooling on wire racks, several hours had passed... and so had the bulk of my anger. When the girls moved out to the backyard so Mia could show off her soccer skills, Liza and I sat companionably on the patio to watch them.

"They look happy," Liza said with a wistful smile. "Really happy."

"They are," I agreed with a surge of pride. "They love their new school. Jacey has already gotten a role in the fall play, which is her dream come true. Cleo was bored to tears at the old school and would have placed out of their math offerings by eighth grade. Mia probably would have been fine staying behind, but it's easier with them all in the same place."

"You don't have to sell me on it, babe," she said with a chuckle. "I trust you to make decisions like that. It's clear you've done a great job with them."

"I couldn't have done it alone," I reminded her. "Not without sacrificing my dedication to my patients. Gwen helped out at first, and then Brody came into our lives..."

"Ah, yes. *Brody*," she said wryly.

"Our girls are thriving, thanks to him," I said sharply. "I'm not sure why you're being so antagonistic towards him—"

"Don't you?" After a moment, she shook her head. "No, I suppose you don't. I forgot who I was dealing with for a second there."

I frowned, and Liza sighed. "I came back because I had a heealth scare," she said. When I leaned forward in my chair, she held up a restraining hand. "Calm down. I'm fine. They thought I had a heart defect, but after a re-scan, they determined it was just a bad scan and assured me I was okay. And before you say anything, I'm already booked in for a checkup here with Dr. Iver." She lifted a knowing eyebrow at me and let out a laugh when I exhaled and nodded my approval.

Liza reached over to squeeze my arm. "It just made me realize I don't want to be far away from the girls anymore. When I first left, I was convinced there was something bigger and better out there for me. But after that scare, I began to realize that I was missing precious time with the people I love. The girls. *You*."

"Liza," I began, shaking my head.

She continued. "Look, I'm not saying I'm sticking around town permanently, but at least if I found some projects to work on in California or even in the States, I'd be able to be in your lives regularly."

"That would be good. Especially for the girls." Although I would have a hard time sharing time with them now that I'd gotten used to only sharing them with her a few weeks a year. "But you and I... you remember I'm gay, right?"

Liza nodded. "Of course. I wasn't expecting that we'd get remarried or share a bed, for heaven's sake. But I did think maybe I could stay here for a while, with all of us under one roof." She sat back in her chair, crossed her legs, and gave me a sardonic smile. "I wasn't expecting that you'd have had a midlife crisis and marry the nanny since the last time we spoke."

"He's a full-time childcare specialist," I muttered. "At least, he *was*."

"Not the point, Grant. How the heck did that happen? Has work been *that* stressful?"

I looked out at the girls and debated my answer. I didn't want to tell Liza the truth about my arrangement with Brody, but I'd known her a long time, and I wasn't used to keeping secrets from her. And more than that, I wanted a gut check. Last night had been so wonderful—so unexpectedly, almost impossibly wonderful—that now, hours later, I found myself questioning it. Was I missing a crucial emotional... *something*? Had I, for once in my life, been too impulsive? Wasn't it all a bit too good to be true?

You couldn't really find your life partner by accidentally convincing them to marry you as part of a business deal...could you?

"I really like him," I admitted, twisting my wedding band with my thumb. "I've had feelings for him for a long time—"

"Lust," she said knowingly. "Physical attraction."

"No! I mean, yes, but not just that. I..." I swallowed hard. "I love him."

"But... how?" she asked, mystified. "What could you possibly have in common? He's a college kid, Grant. Practically a newborn baby."

"Shush. Brody's hardworking, smart, and successful," I said, peeved at her for being so dismissive and equally peeved at my own rush to defend him. "More than that, he's loving and kind. He's helped me to be a better parent. A better doctor. A better person. And he loves the girls like they're his own."

"But they're not. Yes, he's an excellent *nanny*," she allowed, "but you can't ignore the fact that he's still at the very beginning of his adult life. He's not their father. And no matter how magical he is with the children, that doesn't make him the right person to be your life-long partner, either. Surely you see how ridiculous that would be. And aside from all that, as your friend, I have to wonder what his angle is. What's he hoping to get from you?"

I sighed. "Liza, you're coming at this the wrong way. It's not like that—"

"Are you sure?" She gave me a sympathetic grimace. "Because anyone can see the two of you have a passion. Hell, in ten years together, you never kissed me the way you kissed him back there—" She hooked a thumb toward the kitchen. "—or acted all possessive and protective like you do with him. And if you think I'm feeling petty and jealous about that, even though you're gay as fuck and our relationship has been over for years, you're damn right. But maybe Brody's using that. You wouldn't be the first man to be seduced by a good-looking younger guy who—"

"He didn't seduce me!" I darted a glance at the girls to make sure they hadn't heard my outburst, then scrubbed a frustrated hand through my hair and lowered my voice. "If anything, I seduced him. It started out as a necessity, to keep the girls at Mountbatten..."

Slowly, haltingly, I told Liza the full story. About the school, Brody's dreams of starting his own company after graduation, and finally, about crossing the line between fake and real the night before.

Her eyes grew wider and more troubled as I spoke. "Grant. Jesus," she said when I was done. "You need to let the kid go."

My heart dropped. "What? But why?" Everything inside of me railed against the idea. I didn't want to *ever* let Brody go. Not now that I had him.

"Can't you see he didn't have a choice but to say yes?" She shook her head. "You said yourself how much he loves the girls. He wasn't going to break their hearts by refusing to participate in this."

A sick lump lodged in my throat. I felt like I was choking on it. "No, neither of us chose that part, I agree. But he has feelings for me, too. Real feelings." I couldn't doubt that after what we'd shared. "What happened last night... He chose that. I swear he did."

"Of course he did." Liza leaned forward and laid her hand on my knee. "And I'm sure he wouldn't have stayed all these years if he didn't love you all very much. But that doesn't mean you'll be good together long-term." She chewed on her lip for a moment, then said quietly, "Look at what happened with you and me. We fell into a situation neither of us chose when I got pregnant with Jacey way too young, and we committed to each other before we really knew what we wanted out of life. It was good at first—I loved you, and I know you loved me, too, in your way. I thought we could both be happy. It took me years to figure out that I *wasn't*—that you weren't giving me what I needed—and it turned out you weren't being fulfilled, either. We got ourselves stuck, and we had to destroy everything we'd built in order to unstick ourselves."

My stomach gave a sickening lurch. Oh, god. Was that what this was? A repeat of what Liza and I had gone through all those years ago? Was I trapping Brody into this life the way Liza had felt trapped?

Forcing him into a relationship with a man who couldn't give him what he needed emotionally?

How many times had I told myself it was a good thing Brody and I weren't in a relationship because if we were, he would have left long ago?

"Ah, shit. I hate putting that look on your face. Maybe I'm wrong," Liza said quickly. "Petty jealousy aside, I truly hope I am. But now that I'm here, you should offer him a way out, just in case. Make sure he's in it for the right reasons and not because of guilt or obligation, okay?"

She was right. If Liza was going to be around, that would take care of the Mountbatten part of things. Then I could offer Brody his freedom from me. If he wanted it.

Hopefully, he'd laugh in my face and tell me he wanted this like I did.

And on the off chance he didn't? Well, I'd have to figure out a way to get him back or die trying.

Because now that I'd had a taste of him, of what our life could be like together, I wasn't going to let it go without a hell of a fight.

10

———————

BRODY

"You're overreacting," Fen said before shoving a giant spoonful of chocolate ice cream in her mouth.

I hugged the pint of live-saving chocolate to my chest, curled deep into my corner of Fen's sofa, and took another giant spoonful. "Nope. You didn't see Liza earlier. She's gorgeous and sexy and accomplished and great with the girls, and... did I already say gorgeous? Doesn't matter, because it bears repeating. *Gorgeous.* Grant even agreed when I asked him about it."

Fen nodded sagely. "Sure. Grant, the *gay* husband you engaged in *gay* sex with last night, agreed that the *ex*-wife he *divorced* because he's *gay*, was good-looking. It's a calamity. I see that now."

"The girls adore her," I whispered, tears filling my eyes. "They're a perfect little family with her there."

"They're a perfect little family with you there, too. And didn't you tell me he kissed you with *intent* before you left today? That doesn't exactly say, 'Sorry, Brody, it's over,' does it?"

Fen was missing the point entirely. "You were right, all those weeks ago," I admitted. "You told me I was deluding myself into thinking the Brightons were mine, and I was gonna end up miserable—"

"That is *not* what I said. I said you couldn't keep going doing the unrequited love thing. But you and Dr. Schmexy are married now—"

"Not really," I said in a small voice.

"Yes, really." Fen leaned forward and swiped my ice cream away because she was cruel like that. "You consummated it. You licked him, so now he's yours, and Liza can pound sand."

I shook my head. "It doesn't work that way. And maybe it's for the best. If she's moving back here, she can fulfill the stupid requirement at school, and I can just... *ughhh*."

I clutched my stomach. The idea of leaving Grant and the girls made me feel like I was going to get a revisit from the obscene amount of ice cream I'd consumed, but I could tell by my brief interaction with Liza that she would be unsupportive of my relationship with her ex-husband. And was it even a relationship when it included four years of boss/employee and only one real night of more?

"Enough." Fen stood up and yanked the spoon out of my grip, then returned it and the ice cream to her kitchen. "Enough ice cream. Enough feeling sorry for yourself."

"I'm not," I muttered under my breath. I thought about it for a moment. "Or... okay, maybe I am. I'm just... I'm tired of losing people I love, Fen. It hurts."

Fen's face softened. "I know, babydoll." She nudged my feet aside so she could plop back into her spot on the far side of the couch. "I do know. But this isn't remotely like what happened with your family. And what you're doing right now—letting your brain convince you that losing the Grant and the Brightons is inevitable—isn't helping. You're not going to lose them unless your own fear and insecurity makes you push them away. You don't really believe Grant wants his ex-wife, do you? And do you *truly* think she's trying to get back together with him, knowing that he's gay and married?"

I huffed. "No. Not actually. But do I think Grant's smart enough to realize that having a brilliant, beautiful, award-winning photographer doing the parent volunteer hours at Mountbatten might open more doors for the girls than a twenty-four-year-old who's still working on his degree? Probably. And do I worry he might decide he doesn't need an in-name-only husband slash full-time childcare specialist hanging around anymore? Maybe, yeah. And do I think Liza's possessive and protective of all of them and wants to secure her place in the family by pushing me out? No doubt." I shrugged. "The worst part is, I can't even fault her. I might feel the same if they were my kids."

"Those *are* your kids," Fen grumbled. "Who took Mia to the ER when she had that bad ear infection? Who ran Cleo's book report to the school when she left it behind? Who got Jacey pads the first time she got her period? Those are your insecurities talking, babydoll. Dr. McHotstuff wouldn't have taken you to bed if he felt that way about you, would he?"

I didn't think so, but I couldn't say for sure. My head throbbed, and my eyes burned with unshed tears. "Can we change the subject, please? This isn't helping."

"What you need is a plan." Fen crossed her arms defiantly. "A plan to show Dr. Brighton what he'd be missing if he let you go."

"No. No plans. I've had way too much ice cream to think about that right now." I stretched out my legs over her lap. "Do you mind if I stay here for a bit? Things were tense at the house earlier with me there, and that isn't good for the kids. It's probably best if I lie low until Liza, Grant, and I can sort things out."

Fen pinched my leg. "I thought you were instructed to be home tonight."

"Yeah." I gave her a half smile. "But being around that tension's not great for *me*, either."

"In that case, of course you can stay the night." She patted my foot. "And... look on the bright side," she said, suddenly smiling widely. "We can dig in and get some work done so we're ahead of schedule with our classes this semester! That way, when Dr. Brighton calls and tells you to stop being a dumbass—which he will—you won't have to put him off to work on your project."

"We can do that," I agreed.

I did my best to focus on work the rest of the day and tried not to notice when day turned to night. Grant did text and call several times, but I ignored his messages. When I talked to him about what my future with his family would look like, I wanted to be calm and reasonable rather than a torn-up mess. It wasn't Grant's fault I'd fallen for him, and I didn't want him to feel guilty or regret anything that had happened between us.

When my phone buzzed again after midnight, though, an hour after Fen had gone to bed and I'd finally given in to the tears that had been threatening all day, I couldn't ignore it. Something could have been wrong with one of the girls, or the house, or... or...

"Grant?" I croaked, voice broken from crying. "Is everything okay?"

His voice made the hairs on my skin perk up. "No, everything is *not* okay. My husband is missing. My husband, who said he'd come home tonight. Who said he'd text me."

I could hear the worry and sadness in his voice, and I'd be lying if I said it didn't soothe something inside me to know he missed me, too. "I'm sorry I didn't reply to your messages. I just wanted to give us all some space—"

"I don't fucking want space. I want *you*. Here. Now. In our bed." He took a deep breath. "But if that's not what you want, Brody... If anything I said or did at any time made you feel obligated to—*fuck*."

Him talking about *our* bed squeezed my heart in the best way. I imagined him pulling at his shirt collar in frustration as he grasped for words, and thinking of that familiar gesture made a little seed of happiness bloom in my chest where only doubt and sadness had been before.

"Look, I know Liza showing up unannounced wasn't ideal," he went on. "And I'm guessing it brought up a lot of, uh... emotions? Sadness and loss? Thoughts of your parents and brother?"

"Actually... yes," I managed to whisper. "In a way, it did."

"Right. Okay. And that's... that's why you can't come home?"

"At least for tonight," I agreed carefully. "Besides, I have a meeting with Professor Casteel before class in the morning, and you have that patient consult—"

"You promised Cleo you'd come to her robotics thing after school tomorrow," Grant reminded me. "Will you be there?"

"Of course," I said without a second thought. "If Cleo wants me to be."

"She does. And so do I."

Grant spoke with such conviction I couldn't doubt it.

He blew out a breath. "Please, Brody, talk to me. Are you okay?" His voice was softer now, more gentle and hesitant. So damned kind.

"Not really," I said softly, surprising myself with honesty.

"What can I do? How can I fix this?" Grant's voice sounded stressed. "Send me Fen's address, and I'll come get you. I know I'm not anyone's idea of an emotional support person, but I'd like to try. To... to be there for you."

I squeezed my eyes closed and wondered how I'd gotten lucky enough to meet someone who cared enough to want to go into battle for me.

"You're wrong," I whispered. "No one's ever been as supportive of me as you have. But I... I don't think I'm ready to talk tonight. I need rest more than anything, and if we talk, I won't get any."

More than that, I was scared of what might come out of my mouth if we talked right now. Scared I'd beg him to love me. Scared I'd do something to run Liza off, which would disappoint the girls. Scared I'd ruin their family dynamics and make the girls question who they should come to with their issues.

The situation was far more complex than a simple question of what I wanted... or what Grant wanted, either.

Grant exhaled. "Will you call or text if you change your mind? Your number is set to break through my Do Not Disturb setting. I can be there any hour. Promise me."

I nodded, though he couldn't see. "I promise."

"Okay, good. Good. Okay." Grant snorted. "Christ, I sound like an idiot. You know... I became a doctor so I could fix things," he said quietly. "Make people better. I hate that I can't do that for you right now."

"You have." Just talking to him for a few moments made me feel settled in a way I hadn't all day. "Really, Grant."

He paused for a long moment, during which neither of us spoke, and the air around me buzzed with the things I wanted to say but couldn't bring myself to yet.

Like, *I love you.*

Like, *I want this to be real so badly.*

Like, *I want to fight for you. For my family.*

"I'll let you sleep," Grant said finally. "But call me if you... Oh. Uh. Guess I already said that, huh?" He laughed softly. "Good night, sweetheart."

He ended the call before I could say anything, but I could tell I was wearing a goofy smile on my face as I put the phone down. Anything I would have said in return would have sounded as goofy and giddy as I felt.

Maybe Fen was right. Maybe I had overreacted to Liza's sudden appearance.

Grant cared about me. That much was obvious. And it was nice to hear he was also a little mixed up about things like I was. Tomorrow, we'd talk about it, clear the air. And maybe, just maybe, we could find a way to make it work.

I fell into an exhausted but peaceful sleep, imagining that I'd be back in Grant's arms the following day.

But I should have known it wouldn't be quite that easy.

11

GRANT

"And since when do we listen to Liza?" my sister, Gwen, demanded in a low voice so the parents around us couldn't hear. We were standing on the edge of a wide, grassy robotics practice field—a thing I'd swear could only be found at Mountbatten—surrounded by groups of excited kids from several other schools and a collection of robots that were about to do battle... or something like that.

"Since she made a good point. Brody deserves to know he has an out," I said determinedly. What I did not say was that I was equally determined to make sure he didn't take it. I wanted Brody to *want* our marriage to be real, to make that choice of his own free will, but I was prepared to be very convincing.

At least... I hoped I was prepared. I'd tossed and turned all night, organizing my thoughts, and when I'd finally woken from a fitful sleep around dawn, I'd resorted to arranging my thoughts on flash cards, just like I had in med school, to be sure I didn't miss any salient points.

First, though, I needed Brody to show up. I needed to see him with my own eyes and reassure myself that he was alright. I searched the parking lot again for a sign of his arrival, but he wasn't there.

Thankfully, I was distracted from my thoughts by the man next to me muttering under his breath. "What are parents supposed to do at a robotics competition? Cheer? Scream at our team's robots to kick those other kids' robots' asses? What?"

The man he was with said, "Blue, baby, simmer down and just watch, okay?"

"I'm here to support our child, Tristan, and you already took away my poster board sign and my pom-pom, and my emergency pom-pom, too—"

"Mmhmm. We talked about this in the car. Ella specifically asked you to chill after last time."

I was desperate to avoid my sister's interrogation, so I feigned interest in the men's conversation. "I have to ask... what happened last time?"

The man closest to me—Blue—had strawberry blond hair, a mischievous grin, and an abundance of freckles. "I had T-shirts made."

"Don't ask," Tristan said with a sigh. "My husband thinks he's hilarious."

My ears perked up when I realized the two of them were another same-sex parent couple. "No, I need to know. What did the shirts say?"

"Uh." Blue shot a quick glance at his husband and flushed. "I Like Big Bots and I Cannot Lie?"

I burst out laughing.

Blue grinned once again and shot his hand out to shake. "Blue Marian. You're new, aren't you?"

I nodded and shook his warm grip. "Dr. Grant Brighton. My daughter Cleo is the one baring her teeth at the angry kid with the high ponytail."

The man with Blue offered his hand. "I'm Blue's husband, Tristan. That kid with the high pony is ours." His grin was both teasing and understanding.

I winced. "Sorry. Cleo takes her robotics seriously. It's one of the reasons we joined Mountbatten." I gestured toward my sister. "This is Gwen—"

"I'm Grant's sister," Gwen interrupted, grabbing my elbow. "And my brother is currently trying to weasel his way out of an important conversation."

"Oh, really— Wait." Blue leaned in and lowered her voice. "Are you the doctor who married his nanny? Because if so, I owe you a huge thanks for taking the heat off me with the gossipmongers this week."

"That's me." My face heated, but when I caught sight of the man stepping out of his car in the parking lot, I couldn't feel anything but pride and giddy relief. "To be fair, *that*—" I pointed across the grassy area toward Brody. "—is my husband."

Blue and Tristan both turned and stared as Brody made his way toward us. The afternoon sun shone on his wavy brown hair and handsome angular face. My heart raced with excitement like it had been years since I'd set eyes on him instead of a day.

"Uh-huh," Blue said before pursing his lips. "No wonder the ladies couldn't shut up about it."

His husband elbowed him in the side. "Stop drooling. You're embarrassing yourself," he muttered.

Blue turned with a laugh and smacked a kiss on his husband's mouth. "I love you, but I think we need to talk about this sudden need I have for some help with the kids."

"Jackass." Tristan pinched his husband's ass where only I could see it. The two of them were clearly very much in love, which filled me with a strange kind of envy I'd never really felt before.

"Always appreciate an 'I love you, but,'" Tristan added under a laugh.

Because I couldn't take my eyes off Brody, I noticed right away when he stopped ten feet away and gave me an uncertain look, like maybe he wasn't sure he was welcome.

Silly man. As though there could ever be a time when I wouldn't be proud to have him beside me.

"Hey!" I called, unable to restrain my smile as I waved him over. When he strode up, I couldn't help myself. I stepped forward and took him into my arms, dropping a kiss on his lips before pulling him against me. "Hey," I exhaled against his hair in relief. My arms tightened involuntarily. "Hey," I whispered again like a fool.

"Hi," he said softly into my shoulder.

He didn't smell like the organic oatmeal and honey soap he used at home, and I hated that, but underneath, he still smelled like Brody, and I inhaled him like oxygen.

"Missed you," I said roughly.

My sister made an impatient noise, and Brody pulled away from me shyly. When he noticed Blue and Tristan standing beside us, the tops of his ears went pink, and his eyes flicked everywhere but at me. "Um. Hi. And hi, Gwen."

My sister, bless her, grabbed Brody into a big hug. "Hey, sweetie. Mia was asking for you every two minutes, and Grant's been keeping one eye on the parking lot. Now the family's all here."

Brody's blush traveled from his ears down his neck. "Thanks," he said softly.

I cleared the emotion from my throat. I sometimes envied how easily and perfectly Gwen was able to express her feelings. "Brody, this is Blue and Tristan. Their daughter is on the robotics team with Cleo."

They welcomed Brody with warm smiles and friendly chatter, congratulating him on our marriage and asking him questions about himself until Brody managed to get them talking about themselves and their kids. It turned out the two of them owned and managed a vineyard, which automatically made them Gwen's new best friends. Their easy, open conversation made them even more attractive than they already were, which made me stupidly wonder if Brody somehow wished he'd landed one of those guys instead of me.

I wasn't sure I'd ever understood jealousy until Brody came into my life. Now, apparently, I felt it whenever he talked about the cute guy at his gym or even had a friendly conversation with a happily married couple at a school event. It was utterly illogical but also *debilitating*, and I knew the insecurity wouldn't go away until Brody and I had settled things between us. Until I knew he wanted me, permanently, as much as I wanted him.

I blinked at him as he stood in the sunlight, utterly charming everyone around him without even trying, and a revelation hit me like a lightning bolt.

Did Brody know how much I wanted him?

It seemed impossible to me that he wouldn't. I knew my eyes tracked him whenever he was near, that I hung on his every word when he spoke, and I'd made it clear how badly I craved him in my bed... But I remembered his uncertainty Saturday at soccer, his hesitation as he approached me earlier, and the way he'd automatically removed himself from our family activities yesterday like he was an afterthought. Was it possible he felt as unsure as I did?

Gwen would probably smack me for missing something so obvious for so long, but now that I had, I couldn't wait to get Brody alone.

Just as I was about to make my move to extract Brody and myself from the conversation so we could speak privately, Liza joined us from where she'd been chatting with some of the other Mountbatten moms.

"There you are, Grant! Looks like you're over here making friends without me." She smiled at Blue and Tristan, completely ignoring Brody. "You must be the Marians. I've heard quite a bit about you from a couple of the Mountbatten moms—Meera and Candy."

"You mean Candace," Brody corrected quietly. "She was president of the PTA at the girls' old school, and one of her kids is friends with Mia."

Liza visibly bristled and flicked a glance in Brody's direction. "Close enough." She shrugged.

"Actually." Brody gave her a rueful little smile. "I got her name wrong once, four years ago, and she put me in charge of the school's pet parade that spring. I promise, if you'd had to wrangle seven pure-bred corgis, three rottweilers, two ferrets, seventeen cats, and a parakeet on a march around the school grounds, you wouldn't make that mistake twice."

Blue, Tristan, and Gwen laughed out loud, and Liza's expression thawed several degrees.

"Candace, then," she repeated. "I'll learn."

"Brody can help you," Gwen said pointedly.

I reached for Brody and wove our fingers together, then lifted his hand to press a kiss over his wedding band.

I felt the surprise jolt through him at this public display of affection, and that only made me more confident that Brody needed reassurance... and that I really needed to get him alone so I could offer him his freedom and hope like hell he refused it.

Brody's gaze drifted over my shoulder toward the field, and he immediately wrenched his hand from my grip.

"Cleo!" he shouted, bolting out onto the field.

What?

Despite being trained and experienced in medical trauma and known for being cool under pressure, it took me several more seconds to process what was happening. It wasn't until Brody had reached Cleo, dispersing the children who'd clustered around her, that I noticed Cleo's hand was caught in part of her robot, and blood dripped down her arm onto the grass.

"Liza, call for an ambulance. Gwen, grab my bag from the car," I shouted, remembering to toss her the keys from my pocket. I took off after Brody, who was already kneeling in the grass beside my daughter.

"It's okay, baby," he murmured calmly to her as he raised his arm to support her in case she fainted. He braced the forearm of her trapped hand and glanced frantically around. "Grant? Grant!"

I knelt next to them and carefully determined the least damaging way to get her hand unstuck from the gear it was caught in. "Hang on, sweetheart," I said, hoping my voice didn't sound as shaky as I felt. "Take slow breaths, and lean into Brody. He's got you."

The robotics teacher knelt on Cleo's other side, apologizing frantically and holding out a selection of tools to determine which could help remove the gear from the contraption. I grabbed a screwdriver and quickly unscrewed the gear from its housing before it loosened enough to release Cleo's hand. Meanwhile, Brody continued to speak in soothing tones, reassuring Cleo she was okay, telling her how brave she was, and assuring her that her dad was the best doctor in the area.

Right now, her dad felt like a fumbling idiot, but thankfully, Gwen showed up with my medical kit, and I focused on the steps needed to get her wound stabilized so we could transport her to the hospital for X-rays and sutures. The skin was torn, alternately bleeding and white where her hand had been pinched between the teeth. I racked my brain, trying to decide which hand specialist I trusted most with her care.

Sirens indicated the ambulance was approaching. Thankfully, Liza seemed to be in the parking lot directing them rather than hovering in the crowd that had gathered around Cleo. I cleaned the wound and bandaged it temporarily to help control the bleeding and keep it clean while we transported her to the hospital. I knew as soon as I arrived at the emergency room, professional protocol would force me to take a step back and let the trauma surgeon on shift take over her care.

Who was it? Who would be the physician in charge?

"Dad?" Jacey's terrified voice cut through my mental scrambling. She raced over hand in hand with Mia from the school's playground. "What happened? Is she okay?"

The EMTs arrived at the exact same time, with Liza frantically explaining what had happened. The robotics teacher stood up to give them room to begin assessing Cleo.

"She needs to go to the ER," I explained to Jacey as calmly as possible. Poor Mia's eyes were wide as saucers. "She'll be okay, but we need to take a look with the equipment at the hospital to be sure. Aunt Gwen will take you girls home, and I'll call as soon as I have more information."

Cleo was trying to be brave, crying into Brody's sleeve and clutching his arm with her free hand. He was amazing, holding and comforting her without babying her while explaining the situation to the EMTs.

I took over, using more specific language about the possible compression fracture of her fourth and fifth metacarpals and the laceration caused by the sharp gears. When they indicated it was time to load her into the ambulance, Brody offered to carry her since she was basically already in his arms.

It wasn't until he'd set her inside the ambulance and tried to find a seat next to her that we both realized Liza had already taken the only one available for a parent.

"No," I said, gesturing her out. "I'll go with her. I know her medical history, and I have her insurance information. You two take my car. Gwen has the keys."

It wasn't until hours later, when X-rays had shown no evidence of fracture and Cleo's hand had been stitched up by one of the best in the business, that I realized Brody hadn't arrived at the hospital with Liza.

"Where is he?" I asked my ex-wife, peering behind her into the ER waiting room as we accompanied Cleo in the wheelchair to the exit doors. "Didn't Brody ride with you?"

She shook her head. "He had his own car. Said he knew Cleo was in good hands."

My phone buzzed in my pocket, and I saw a text from Brody.

BRODY

Sorry to bother you, but I wanted to see if Cleo's okay?

My heart dropped as I tapped out a response. This miscommunication needed to end. I hated hearing Brody sound unsure of his role in our family.

ME

She's fine, but I'm not. Are you at home?

12

———————

BRODY

I stared down at the message from Grant as my heart began to bang in my chest.

Fen peered over my shoulder. "Told you so."

"Stop. He just wants to make sure Mia and Jacey aren't alone." I quickly typed a response.

The three dots swirled beside Grant's name for a long moment, then disappeared altogether.

"See?" I said, gesturing with the phone. "Grant's busy. He's got a lot going on, taking care of his family, and that's where his focus is. *As it should be.* We'll sort things out later."

"Okay, I was willing to be sympathetic yesterday, boo," Fen said, grabbing the phone from my hand. "But you're making a mistake. Dr. Love Machine has had a bad scare. He needs you. They all do."

I shook my head. "I'm not going to burden him with all this drama. Not when he's already been dealing with Cleo and emotions are high."

"That is *exactly* when he needs you most, you freaking idi—*oooh*."

Fen's insult cut off when my phone buzzed in her hand, and both of us glanced down at Grant's message.

I blinked at the screen, and my heart thundered up into my throat. "He's mad," I whispered, standing up on shaky legs and gesturing toward the door. "I should probably—"

"You should *definitely*." Instead of being concerned about me like a true friend, Fen simply grinned. "Angry comfort sex for the win. Get it, babydoll."

I really doubted Grant Brighton was in any mood for sex, but clearly, he was ready to have things out with me, one way or another. And although the way he'd taken pains to include me at the robotics field had made me feel warm and hopeful, there was nothing like a family emergency to remind everyone who the actual parents in the situation were.

Who the actual *family* members were.

Those girls were Grant and Liza's daughters, not mine.

I held my emotions in check while I drove over to the house. Then, as uncomfortable and awkward as it was, I forced myself to ring the doorbell instead of letting myself in.

Jacey answered the door. Her forehead crinkled in confusion. "Why are you ringing the bell? Did you forget your keys or something?"

"Brody's being an idiot," Grant's voice sounded from somewhere in the living room. "He thinks he's a guest in our home now."

Jacey's eyes narrowed with teenage scorn. "A guest? Since when?"

I ignored this and stepped inside. "How's Cleo? Can I see her?"

She nodded and pointed toward the living room. When I came around the corner, I saw the reason Grant hadn't greeted me in the foyer and called me names face-to-face. Poor Cleo was curled up in a ball with her head on his lap. Grant's hand brushed through her short, wavy hair, and her bandaged hand lay propped up on a pillow next to her. Her eyes were half-lidded and glazed. Liza was nowhere to be found.

I moved to kneel in front of her, ignoring Grant's presence as much as I could. "Hey, sweet girl. How are you? Are the meds keeping the pain away?"

I reached out to brush her hair out of her eye, accidentally brushing my fingers against Grant's. Our eyes met for a second, but I looked away before I could decipher the emotion in his expression.

Cleo's eyes began to leak. "Brody, where were you? Dad said you'd make me cinnamon chocolate milk when we got home, but you weren't here."

Oh, god. My chest felt like it was going to cave in. "I'll make it right now, love. Stay right here." I stood up but froze as soon as Grant reached out to grab my wrist.

"Make it small. She needs something in her stomach, but I don't want her to have too much. She's going to pass out in a minute when the meds fully kick in."

I nodded and raced to the kitchen, moving by rote memory through the steps to make her the special drink. When I got back to the living room, Grant had sat her up and propped her against the back of the sofa.

"Here you go. Let me help," I said, sitting on her other side to make sure the drink didn't spill. As soon as she'd finished it, her eyes drooped more, and Grant stood with her in his arms to carry her to bed.

"Wait, Dad," Cleo mumbled as he began to move away. "Brody, will you be here to make more chocolate milk tomorrow morning?"

I pressed a hand to the ache behind my breastbone. I hated that she doubted that for a single second. That I was the one who'd made her doubt it by not being there when she needed me. I'd promised

Jacey that I would never walk away from my girls, so it was beyond time for me to put my fears aside.

"Yes, sweetheart. Of course I will."

"M'kay." Cleo cuddled deeper into Grant's chest. "G'night, then. Love you."

"Love you, too," I said, covering my breaking heart with as much of a smile as I could muster.

Grant pinned me with an intense glare. "Wait for me in my office while I check on the other girls. Do not leave."

I nodded. I headed across the hall to his office and took a seat on the small sofa where I'd sat when Grant interviewed me four years ago... the same spot where he'd asked me to be his husband just a few weeks back. So much had changed since then, but the most essential ones had not. I wanted this house to be my home. I wanted the Brightons to be my family.

I wanted to belong here.

When Grant returned to the living room, he closed the door behind him and assessed me for a long moment, his jaw tight.

I gripped my fingers in my lap so tightly they turned white, and my mind blanked. Should I apologize first, or beg for another chance, or—

"What the fuck were you thinking?" Grant barked.

I jumped in my seat. "I... I'm so sorry, Gr—Dr. Brighton. I screwed up. I should have... I should have—"

Before I could get another word out of my mouth, Grant pulled me up from my seat and crushed his mouth to mine. The move shocked the breath out of me, and all I could do was clutch at his shirt while his arms wrapped tightly around me.

"*Not* Dr. Brighton," he said roughly against my lips. "Not to you. Not anymore." He touched his forehead to mine. "Tell me you want this, Brody. Tell me you want *me*."

"I don't understand," I said, gasping for breath at the same time I was straining on my tiptoes, trying to push myself closer, wanting as much contact with him as I could get. "Of course I do."

"Then why did you leave us? Why did you go back to Fen's when we needed you, when *I* needed you?"

He kissed me again, even harder than before, but didn't wait for an answer. Instead, words started pouring out of him between rough, possessive kisses, blanketing my senses. "Fuck. I had a whole speech prepared. I had flash cards. I wanted to tell you that you're not obligated to stay married to me anymore if you don't want to, now that Liza's back to help out with Mountbatten, and then I planned to list all the practical reasons why I hoped you'd choose to stay with me anyway, like being there for the girls and keeping your health insurance. But fuck practicality. Fuck obligation. You can be with the girls as much as you want, forever, no matter what you choose," he promised.

He pulled back just far enough to cradle my jaw in both of his hands. "This conversation is about *us*. And what it comes down to, Brody, is that I *need* you. I fucking need you. I need your sunshine and your passion, your understanding and your patience, your calmness when chaos strikes. I want you with me every day, as my husband, making pancakes and eating all the leftover pizza when I buy too much. Telling me ridiculous stories about Fen and your professors. Making my life better in a thousand tiny ways. Letting me take care of you, even when you don't need it. I need you to tell me, right now, what *you* want."

Once again, he didn't give me a chance to tell him much of anything. His arms went back around me, and his mouth trailed hot kisses over my jaw and neck.

"Oh god," I breathed, so stunned and *wanting* that no other words would emerge. The things he was saying, the things he was *doing*... "I didn't expect this. N-not any of it," I stammered.

Because maybe Fen was right. In my head, in my heart, I'd accepted the idea that loving people meant losing them. And while that hadn't stopped me from falling for Grant or his daughters, it had stopped me from trusting that it could ever end happily.

Christ, I'd been an idiot.

Grant pushed me away and held me at arm's length. His stare was intense enough to light an inferno in my lower belly. "Talk to me. Spell it out for me. No more halfways. No more misunderstandings."

My legs felt like jelly. Without him holding on to me, I fell back down on the sofa like a rag doll. "I'm so sorry—" I began again.

Grant let out a frustrated noise and lowered to his knees in front of me. "No more apologies, either." He took a deep breath and forced a brave smile, leaning away from me slightly. "And no obligations. If you don't feel the same, just say so—"

Oh, god, no.

"I do!" I exclaimed. I lurched forward and grabbed his face, kissing his forced smile hard enough to wipe it from my memory. "I love you," I blurted into our kiss. "I love you, and I want to be married to you... and I was scared you didn't want me like that. That you were just trying to make the best of an awkward situation. That *you* felt obligated to *me*."

"Oh, god." Grant squeezed his eyes shut and exhaled shakily. "It didn't even occur to me that you could have those same fears until today. I'm afraid I'm a bad bet when it comes to relationships, Brody—"

"You keep saying that," I said sharply. "It's not true. You just laid your heart out for me, and it was *perfect*. You're kind, and thoughtful, and so damn generous, always. You give so much to your sister, and your mother, and your daughters, and your patients. You spend your whole day saving lives, Grant, and then you come home and devote yourself to your family. So don't ever tell me again that you're not good at emotions or good at supporting people. Because maybe you weren't what someone else needed, but you are *exactly* the man I need. The man I want."

Grant frowned like the words were painful... but the emotion shining in his eyes let me know it was the sweetest kind of pain.

He pulled me down onto the floor with him until I was straddling his lap and his arms were wrapped tightly around me again. "I love you, too. So much. I think maybe I've been in love with you all along, ever since you walked into this office four years ago and informed me that you were a—"

"Full-time childcare specialist," we finished together. I laughed, and Grant grinned.

"You make me so damn happy," he said wonderingly. "I feel..." He took a moment to search for the right words. "...unaccountably lucky. Like fate has chosen me as some kind of special winner by having you walk into my life. And I don't ever want to let you go."

I'd never believed I'd find someone who'd say those things to me, and my eyes burned with unshed tears. "I was scared," I admitted, finding that it wasn't difficult at all to tell the truth now that I knew how Grant felt. "Scared you'd change your mind now that Liza's back. Scared I'd lose another family—"

"Ah, baby—" Grant shook his head sympathetically.

"—and scared that I'd get in the way of her relationship with the girls. They deserve to have as much family love as they can."

"But Brody, *you* are their family, too," Grant said, sounding so much like Fen that I knew she'd never let me live it down. "They can't do without you, and neither can I. Besides, Liza and the girls are responsible for their own relationships. You haven't gotten in the way of anything. You've simply loved the girls unconditionally from day one. They know that, and deep down, Liza does, too. She made a hard choice when she left, and even though she's done a decent job of keeping up a relationship with the girls despite the distance, she can't simply come back and expect things to be the way they were before. Jacey, Cleo, and Mia will decide what place they want her to have in their lives. We can guide them, as their dads, but we can't own that for them."

"Dads," I repeated, letting the word sink burrow inside me, filling up all the places that had been hollow since the day I lost my parents and my brother.

"Yeah." Grant smiled knowingly. "What we do have to work on, though, is establishing boundaries. And one of the first ones I'm erecting is a giant wall around you and me, this house, *our home*. No one is allowed to make you feel unwelcome here, ever. And no amount of derision or opinion from Liza or anyone else is allowed to get between you and the girls. The girls wouldn't stand for it, frankly."

His words washed over me, gifting me with everything I'd ever wanted. Family. Love. Acceptance.

"Thank you for telling me to come home," I said softly before pressing another kiss to his lips. "Thank you for loving me and fighting for me."

"Brody Kelly," Grant said, oddly formally. "Will you do me the honor of marrying me? Of spending the rest of your life by my side and allowing me to love, support, and honor you the rest of my days?"

"Didn't we already do this part?" I asked, feeling my cheeks stretch wide with a happy grin.

"I need you to know it's real this time." His smile was softer... affectionate and endearing. I wanted him to take me to bed right this minute.

"I will," I said before leaning in to seal my promise with a kiss.

"Maybe we can have a real wedding this time," he said against my mouth. "Make it a giant party and invite everyone. The girls will love it."

"A dance party?" I grinned. "Absolutely. I agree."

"But no more than *two* Taylor Swift songs," Grant informed me in his best Cleo impression.

"Do I get to play the *love* ones this time?" I teased.

"Always," he said softly, brushing his lips over mine. "As long as you dance with me."

"Baby, why are you shaking?" Brody asked as he pulled off my shirt later that night.

The house was quiet, the girls all asleep in their beds, and I'd called Liza and Gwen half an hour ago to assure them that Cleo was resting comfortably, but when Brody had wrapped an arm around my waist and led me upstairs to my room—our room—I'd begun trembling, and I couldn't seem to stop.

"Adrenaline crash, probably," I diagnosed myself. "I was terrified."

Brody nodded. "I get it. But Cleo's sound asleep," he soothed. "And you said the damage to her hand looked worse than it actually was."

"It's not about Cleo. It's about you," I admitted ruefully. "I told you once before—putting people together is what I'm good at. But when you weren't at the hospital, when I thought maybe I'd lost you for good, I didn't know how to make that better."

Brody slid his hands around my bare torso and leaned his face into my neck. "But you did. You called me, and I came back. And I promise, Grant, I *swear*, I won't leave again."

I nodded against the top of his hair. We'd already made promises to each other downstairs, and I believed him, but apparently, I needed more reassurance. Fortunately, Brody could tell. He held me tighter and breathed me in.

"I'm still ten years older than you," I pointed out. "Liza said maybe I was getting you into a situation like the one she and I were in when we got married, trapping you when you're too young to really know what you want."

Brody snorted softly. "Liza doesn't know me," he pointed out. "Maybe she felt trapped, but I don't feel that way in the slightest. I feel safe. Adored. Cherished. Supported. Wanted. Having you hold me like this... I can't imagine anything more right."

He spoke the words with such quiet conviction that I couldn't doubt him. "So that means I don't have to get in shape to take on the tattooed man at your gym for your affections?"

Brody laughed lightly. "Full confession time: Gym Crush Dude is named Dwayne, and he's married to an equally tattooed woman who's pregnant with their third child. I've never really had a crush on him, and he for sure hasn't looked twice at me, except to ask if I was almost done with the elliptical. I just... didn't want you to realize who I *actually* had a crush on."

"Are you serious?" I snickered. "I was racked with jealousy for nothing?"

He pulled back to stare at me, his green eyes filled with confusion. "You were jealous? *You*?"

"God, yes. I nearly challenged Blue Marian to a duel for you today."

"Who?" he demanded.

I laughed out loud. He didn't even remember the gorgeous redhead's name. "The married couple who own the winery, remember? We watched you walking across the field toward us, looking so freaking delectable in your jeans, with your hair shining in the sun, and I thought his eyes would fall out of his head."

"You're insane. That man is profoundly, stupidly in love with his husband," Brody countered, a slow smile dawning on his face. "I got that within the first minute of our conversation."

"Yes, but so am I," I reminded him, pressing a kiss to the tip of his nose. "And I was very worried you might find one of them more attractive than me."

I was teasing, but it was mostly true. It had been awful, and I was ashamed to even admit it aloud.

He laughed and moved his hands down to unfasten the button on my pants. "Don't get me wrong, those guys were definitely good-looking, but they were nowhere near as hot as my sexy husband."

His emphasis on the final word made me squeeze my eyes closed and breathe deeply. *Thank you for this moment. For this man.*

"You're blind," I said with a soft laugh. "But I love you anyway."

"Not blind," Brody said, shoving my pants down and moving his hands up to cup my ass cheeks over the smooth cotton of my boxer briefs. "While you were busy worrying about those two, I was noticing a cluster of moms from the other school who couldn't keep their eyes off you. You had your damned shirtsleeves rolled up the way that drives me crazy. If it was making *me* hot, I can only imagine—"

I stopped him with a kiss. Happiness filled my body like helium, making me feel nearly buoyant. I'd never felt this purely joyful before, and I was pretty sure that was because I'd never been in love like this before, either.

I'd loved Liza—I still did, as a friend, as the mother of my children, as a person I'd shared a wonderful history with. But now I could see that she and I were very different people who wanted different things, and *that* was what had doomed our relationship, far more than any emotional inadequacy on my part. It had been nothing like the pure sunshine warmth and bone-deep connection I had felt with Brody from the very beginning.

I kissed him while we stood half-naked in the middle of *our* bedroom, where I could continue to seduce and flirt and laugh with him for years to come. Where I could share and cry and strategize with him. Where I would always and forevermore be at home with him.

Thinking about our life together, long and stretched out before us, filled with all the life-changing milestones and magical everyday moments we'd share with the girls and each other, somehow, impossibly, made me even hotter for him.

"Do you know... the day you came here to interview for the nanny job, I almost turned you down?"

He looked up at me, his eyes glazed with lust and his breathing rough. "I figured. I had no experience, and I didn't exactly look the part."

"You looked too much the part." I grazed my teeth over his stubbled chin and felt him shiver in my arms. "Not the part of the full-time childcare specialist, though. I wanted you in my bed even then. I had to stop myself from eyeing you up and down like a greedy bastard and imagining you naked. I resorted to reciting the bones of the human body to stop myself from dropping to my knees. *Calcaneus, talus, metatarsals...*"

"That explains the strangely manic expression on your face," Brody said with a grin. "Meanwhile, I was wondering whether I could catch a glimpse of your ass. I finally got so desperate I asked you for a glass of water. Worth it."

"Oh my god," I said, reaching up to tug on a hank of his hair. "Treating your potential employer like a piece of meat? For shame."

His smile was unapologetic. "You have no idea. I went back to my apartment and jacked off to the memory and figured I was safe because you'd never hire me. When you did, I could barely meet your eyes. I promised myself I'd never masturbate under your roof."

I raised one eyebrow. "How long did that last?"

"Oh, a good long while," he assured me innocently. "At least four hours."

I laughed, letting my hands drift down to cup his luscious ass. "Probably longer than I lasted."

"Once I'd broken the seal on touching myself under your roof, I saw no point in going back."

The image of Brody in his room at my house, wrapping his strong hand around his cock, made my stomach clench. "Fuck, you're killing me."

My hands moved all over his bare skin, mapping his body and relishing in the fact it was mine to possess and cherish now.

Brody did the same, pulling off the remainder of my clothes so he could mark me with his touch. It was sensual and erotic in a way that made me hard as steel. "Want you to fuck me into this bed," he said against the skin on my shoulder, right before his tongue darted out to taste me.

I let out a noise from my throat and wondered whether I'd be able to maintain enough control to even get to that point.

Brody continued teasing me relentlessly. "Do you have any idea how many sexual scenarios I've fantasized about with you?" he murmured. The smirk on his lips disappeared as he leaned down to suck my nipple into his mouth. "Enough to keep us busy for years."

"Can't be more than me," I hissed.

"Bet you it can. I once imagined you fucking me over the hood of a car in the grocery store parking lot. The image flashed in my head one time when the girls were fighting about something and you barked at them in this hot-as-fuck commanding voice. 'Listen to me,' you said. It made me hard right there next to where Mrs. Leonetti was returning her cart."

That surprised a laugh out of me. "You're filthy."

"I guess I am. But you married me." He held up his left hand to show off his ring. "No take-backsies."

I groaned again at the reminder that he was mine... forever. "You're trying to get me to come before I'm even inside you."

"Then hurry up." Brody punctuated his suggestion with a hand on my cock, giving it the perfect amount of grip and squeeze.

I moved him over to the bed, pushing him down on his back so I could lean over and feast on his dick.

"Love you," I said softly between teasing licks and sucks. "I can't believe I get to be the one to do this."

Brody's breathing stuttered as his fingers tugged my hair. "Fuck, that feels so good. Don't stop."

I reached blindly for the lube in the bedside table before uncapping it and slicking up my fingers. When I reached down to find his tight hole, I had to stop and take a breath to keep from humping to completion against the bed between his legs.

"This okay?" I asked as I breached him carefully with my middle finger.

"More. Harder. Don't worry about hurting me."

I met his eyes. "I will always worry about hurting you," I said seriously.

Brody's face softened. "And I love you for that. But I want you to fuck me hard. I want you as close inside me as you can be."

After that, it was like time sped up. I stretched him with my fingers while savoring him with my mouth just enough to keep him on edge.

When I finally slicked up my own shaft and moved up to push inside him, I felt like crying out in relief and amazement. The tight heat of his body, with nothing between us, was the most incredible pleasure I'd ever felt.

"Fuck," I groaned.

Brody's legs came up to cross against my back. "Like that," he gasped. "Oh god. Baby, fuck. Oh, *fuck*."

He threw his head back and groaned as I did my best to nail just the right spot. "Not going to last," I gritted through tight teeth. I wanted this feeling to last forever.

I held on to him as I continued to thrust in and out of his body, cementing the bond we'd forged and declaring him mine in every way.

"*Grant!*" he cried before his body locked down for a split second, and the sound of his hitched breaths accompanied his body's warm release between us.

I finally let go and felt my own release, charging hard and fast up my spine and all the way through my fingers and toes, and as I came, my mind locked on the idea I would get to have this again, and again, and again, until death did us part.

When I finally began to catch my breath, I grinned down at him and found him smiling up at me the same way, like mirror images.

Like two halves of a whole that had improbably, incredibly, through pain and loss and uncertainty, found their way to one another.

"You look like you won the lottery," he teased, running long fingers through my messy hair.

"I think we both did," I agreed, kissing him softly. "And tomorrow, I'm going to send Dean Larson a lovely bouquet of flowers to thank her."

Because never in a million years could I have imagined that a marriage of convenience might be the best thing that ever happened to me...

But it absolutely was.

EPILOGUE TWO
BRODY

"Mattie, stop putting frosting on the dog," Blue said to his son before turning to me and handing me another glass of sparkling wine. "Are you regretting inviting kids to the wedding? Because I sure am."

I took a sip and savored the flavor. "Never. Whenever we're here at the vineyard, I feel like I can just let nature watch the girls for us. What's the worst that could happen?"

Mia ran by with a champagne glass in her hand that I had to hope held only sparkling grape juice.

"*Zzzt*," Blue hissed. "You just jinxed us."

Sure enough, in the next second, a scream split the air. "Sorry," I said, turning to find where the sound originated. Thankfully, it wasn't one of ours. "Whose little boy is that?"

"My sister Simone's youngest." Blue rolled his eyes. "I can tell by the sound that's his fake cry. It's his new favorite thing whenever his father is around. The man is a sucker for tears."

Grant walked up in time to hear the tail end of Blue's statement. "You aren't telling him about last night, are you?" he asked with an accusatory look.

I thought back to the night before. With the approach of our "real" wedding, I'd gotten overwhelmed with emotion, so much I'd actually cried.

"No," I murmured with a smile. "We weren't talking about you."

"We are now, though," Blue said with a knowing grin. "Spill."

Over the past year, we'd become close friends with Blue and Tristan Marian. They had an incredible group of other gay couple family and friends who lived here in Napa, and we found ourselves gravitating toward their group more and more. Their kids had been at Mountbatten longer than ours had, so they were a great resource in navigating some of the challenges that had arisen over our first year at the school.

And, I couldn't lie, the man was a comic genius with his custom T-shirts.

Grant's fingers tangled with mine, and he bumped my shoulder, letting me know he was okay with me sharing a little with Blue.

"It hit me last night that this was finally real," I confessed. "Even after a whole year together, I still can't believe I'm living my fairy tale. So when I overheard him on a phone call referring to me as his 'beloved husband,' I kind of lost it."

Blue gave us a knowing smile. "Isn't it the best? You know the story of how Tristan and I started out pretending to be a couple, right?"

I nodded, having heard the whole hilarious tale of their fake relationship more than once, usually over copious amounts of wine.

Blue's gaze automatically searched out his husband, who stood near the buffet table charming Grant's mother and Fen, and his smile became a huge, satisfied grin. "Even now, after years of being married, when Tristan calls me his husband, it does something to me." He sighed happily before turning his attention back to Grant. "So, who were you telling about your beloved husband?"

"Work," Grant admitted with an eye roll. "They wanted me to cut our honeymoon short to cover a couple of shifts in the ER, and I... disagreed."

"*Forcefully*," I added, my chest puffed with pride the way it had the night before. "You should have heard him. He got that deep, commanding voice that makes me crazy and said, 'I have given this hospital everything for years, but I will not ask my beloved husband to forsake one moment of our family time because of your staffing issues.' I was so proud of him."

"Hot." Blue shot Grant a wink. "Seriously hot."

Grant's cheeks turned pink. "It was time. I started pushing back a while ago, but they didn't get the message. But I know exactly what, and who, my priorities are, and if the hospital doesn't like the boundaries I'm setting, I'll get a new job."

Blue nodded. "Plenty of opportunity to open a general practice here right now. The area is booming." He grinned at me. "And that's what made you cry?"

"Oh yeah. Burst into tears right in front of the girls," I admitted. "Cleo yelled, 'Dad, he's doing it again!' *Pfft*. As if I cry all the time."

Grant's laugh turned into a cough when I elbowed him in the side. He leaned over to press a laughing kiss to my temple. "I love that you never hide your emotions from me. It shows how much you care."

"You do not love it," I argued. "Not always. You said seeing me cry hurts worse than the worst avulsion you've seen in the ER." I looked at Blue. "Do not google that word if you value your stomach contents."

"This is also true," Grant admitted. "Makes me crazy."

"It also makes you *generous*." I winked before looking back at Blue. "Pro tip: cry to Tristan and then ask him to kiss it better. Thank me later."

Blue's laughter brought Tristan over to see what we were talking about. We didn't stick around long enough for him to test my theory, though, because Jacey called us over to the cake table.

"Mom said to make sure you got a piece of the cake," she said, handing us each a plate. "Which makes no sense since you already fed each other a piece when you cut the cake, but whatever. She's, like, your bestie now, so I figured she'd know best."

I wouldn't say Liza and I were besties, exactly, but once Grant and I had cemented our relationship last year, the tension between Liza and me had disappeared almost immediately, too. It turned out she'd been genuinely worried that Grant and I would end up miserable, which would make the girls miserable as well. Once she'd gotten over her shock at our marriage and seen with her own eyes how happy and settled we all were, she had no objections to our relationship. Though she hadn't stayed in town permanently, she'd made an effort to keep her work trips shorter, and we'd fallen into an easy routine as friends and coparents.

As family.

I took a bite of the moist cake and groaned. "Your mother is doing the Lord's work," I admitted. "I told her when she helped me decide on the cake maker that I was worried I wouldn't get to actually enjoy the cake I picked. She said she'd make sure we got plenty."

"Liza said that?" Grant asked, savoring his own bite. "This is incredible."

I nodded. "I told you what a huge help she was when all the final wedding details came to a head at the same time my beta was going live. She came back from her Louisiana trip and threw herself full-tilt into wedding planning. That's how I got her and the girls to make all the favor packets and half the centerpieces."

Grant peered over the crowd to find Liza's blonde hair, which was done up for the wedding. "I'll have to thank her."

Jacey shook her head. "Not now. She's putting the moves on Toby."

"Who's Toby?" Grant asked, squinting to make out the younger man standing with Liza.

I leaned in and lowered my voice. "Tristan's head of distribution here at the vineyard. Total playboy."

"Is it serious?" he asked.

I glanced at Jacey, who was thankfully distracted by a dog who'd come over for pets, and lowered my voice to a whisper. "I believe your ex-wife is simply looking for some... ah... temporary physical entertainment."

His laugh brought a smile to my face. It was one of my favorite sounds in the entire world. "Good for her."

"You're not jealous?" I teased. I had no doubt that Grant was completely committed to me, even before he'd sworn it in front of our friends and family two hours earlier.

"Jealous of someone getting physical entertainment? Hell yes I am. In fact, I want to whisk you off and physically entertain the hell out of you right now," he growled. "What do you say to that plan, Mr. Brighton?"

I looked around at the golden sun shining on our friends and family, at the gorgeous vistas of Alexander Vineyard, at the glinting platinum band on my finger, and grinned. Once upon a time, I'd worried love was a fleeting thing that could be snatched away in a heartbeat. But standing in Grant's arms, I knew down to my soul that, no matter what challenges and joys life had in store for us, our love— our *family*—would last forever. And I would never doubt that again.

I stood on my tiptoes and pressed a kiss to my husband's lips.

"I say... *I do.*"

Thank you for reading The Nanny Proposal*! For the story of how Blue and Tristan fell in love, check out* Borrowing Blue.

Want another boss/employee, forced proximity short story? Get Luca and Marcel *FREE when you sign up for my newsletter: https://readerlinks.com/ l/4183185*

ABOUT LUCY LENNOX

Lucy Lennox is the USA Today bestselling author of over fifty gay romance titles including the GoodReads Hall of Fame winner Wilde Love. Born and raised in the southeast USA, she is finally putting good use to that English Lit degree she earned before the turn of the century.

Lucy enjoys naps, pizza, and procrastinating. She stays up way too late each night reading romance because it's simply the best.

For more information and to stay updated about future releases, sales and audio news and to grab some free and bonus reads, please sign up for Lucy's author newsletter on her website at LucyLennox.com or to stay in the know, join her exciting reader group, Lucy's Lair on Facebook.

facebook.com/lucylennoxmm

instagram.com/lucylennoxmm

amazon.com/Lucy-Lennox/e/Bo1No1OYPT

bookbub.com/authors/lucy-lennox

pinterest.com/lucy_lennox

ALSO BY LUCY LENNOX

Join Lucy's Lair

Get Lucy's New Release Alerts

Like Lucy on Facebook

Follow Lucy on BookBub

Follow Lucy on Amazon

Follow Lucy on Instagram

Follow Lucy on Pinterest

Other books by Lucy:

Made Marian Series

Forever Wilde Series

Aster Valley Series

Virgin Flyer

Say You'll Be Nine

Hostile Takeover

Prince of Lies

Mister Majestic

Twist of Fate Series with Sloane Kennedy

After Oscar Series with Molly Maddox

Licking Thicket Series with May Archer

Champion Security series with May Archer

Honeybridge series with May Archer

Visit Lucy's website at www.LucyLennox.com for a comprehensive list of titles, audio samples, freebies, suggested reading order, and more!